Hearts on the Run

Annie J. Kribs

This book is a work of fiction. Names, characters, places and incidents are works of the author's imagination and are used fictitiously. Similarity to actual people, places and events are entirely coincidental.

All right reserved, including the right to reproduce this book or any portions in any form whatsoever. For information, email anniekribs@gmail.com.

Original Copyright © 2017 by Annie J. Kribs

ISBN: 8444643983
ISBN-13: 9798444643983

Dedication

For Wanda

I'll make a reader of you yet!

Prologue

"Last stop before the Canadian border." The driver's voice crackled over the speaker, startling several of the passengers. Rachel Henige readjusted her position and peered out the condensation covered window. The bus had pulled to a stop outside a sprawling station, passengers bustling in and around the brightly lit building, even though it was the middle of the night. She tried to look beyond the station to see the city but couldn't make out much. She had no idea where she was. Feeling slightly ill, and a lot like she needed a restroom, she stood slowly and wobbled a little as she gained her balance and waited for other passengers to debark the bus.

An older gentleman ushered her ahead of him into the narrow center aisle. She nodded her thanks and gathered her battered backpack in front of her. She wondered if there was such a thing as bus-lag? If so, she definitely had it.

The bus driver waited beside the steps to help each person off of the bus. Rachel joined the small throng of passengers waiting for their bags to be retrieved from beneath the vehicle. Because she'd been the first one on the bus, she received her luggage last. One large, one small suitcase and her backpack. All of her worldly goods could be carried in two arms. It was a far cry from the way she'd been raised. The way she'd lived up until three months ago. She was a realist. She's probably never live that comfortably again and she was at peace with her decision.

The bus driver laid a gentle hand over hers when she reached for her suitcase. "You have someone meeting you here?"

Rachel looked around. She didn't want to admit she didn't even know where *here* was. "No."

The older man studied her with a quiet sort of understanding. "You've been on my bus for several days now. Do you have a destination in mind?" He winked playfully. "Or do you enjoy my company?"

She gave him a grateful smile. "No particular destination, no. I'm travelling cross-country. Seeing the sights."

He nodded once. She could tell he wasn't buying that. "Do you have your passport?"

She did. But she didn't plan to use it. "I'm not heading to Canada."

"Well, that's probably for the best. This is a long trip to be making alone. Do you have family here? I can wait while you call."

She pressed her lips together and shook her head. Damn her crazy hormones. She didn't want to make a fool of herself by crying on this poor sweet stranger.

He nodded again. "Well, as you have no destination in mind, and as I have no plans to smuggle you out of the country, how about if I recommend somewhere warm and cozy to stay for a bit?"

Rachel blinked a few times to force the tears back. "I don't have a lot of money to spend on a hotel, but I would appreciate your suggestions for somewhere safe to stay the night. I'm not at all familiar with the area."

He pulled a weathered suitcase out of the luggage compartment and then closed and locked it. Taking one of her bags with this free hand, he indicated for her to take the lead into the station. "Tell you what. How about if I make a quick call and see if I can't get you a room for the night? We can arrange a cab to get you there lickety-split and soon enough you'll be sound asleep.

That sounded heavenly, if a little scary. "I'll need to know the cost so that I can make a decision first."

One side of his mouth tipped up in a smile. "Of course."

Rachel followed the bus driver to a small table where they could park their luggage and sit for a moment. She mentally tallied her cash and decided on an amount she could spare on a hotel for the night. She would much rather have stayed on the bus another day, but she had to face the facts. She would need to settle somewhere, and soon. She needed to find a job and housing before she blew through the rest of her savings.

The driver, whose name she knew was Randy, pulled out his cell phone and scrolled through his contacts, settling on one and pushed the button to make a call.

"Hey Buzzy. Randy here." He listened and smiled.

"Yes. Your cousin Randy. How many Randys do you know?" He chuckled. "Sorry for calling in the dead of night. Do you have a room free for a day or two? I have a pretty young woman here who sure could use a place to rest and a couple of home-cooked meals."

He stared at Rachel while he listened for a minute. Suddenly he smiled and Rachel couldn't help but sigh in relief. She didn't even know why his smile made her feel better, but it did. All she could do was follow her instincts and pray they were sound.

"Forty-five minutes?" He frowned. "Shave off fifteen and come in your pajamas then." He gave another playful shake of his head and thanked his cousin.

Setting his phone on the table between them, he sat back and smiled. "My cousin Buzzy runs a quaint little bed and breakfast in Wolf Creek. That's about a half hour from here. She has a room available, and is on her way to come pick you up."

Rachel stared at him. "Oh, but." Her stomach took a dive. "You didn't ask the cost."

He was already shaking his head. "You can discuss it with Buzzy, but I suspect she'll get one look at you and take you in." He chuckled. "Prepare to be smothered."

Rachel smiled and it took effort not to show how badly she was shaken. Her choices were slim but her instincts told her to trust him. She was terrified. She was exhausted. She was hungry. And she was saved.

Chapter 1

Ten Years Later

"You need to loosen up a little, Rachel. You take life too seriously." Tilly delivered the familiar criticism with a smile.

"I'm a single parent. I have to take life seriously."

"Because her father is...?" Tilly raised an eyebrow at her, but Rachel knew she didn't really expect an answer. Rachel's past, including Anna's parentage, was nobody's business. Everyone was entitled to their secrets, and as small-town waitresses they both knew everybody had one.

"Even single mothers can have a life, you know."

"I'm not interested in dating." Rachel realized how prim she sounded and sighed. At twenty-nine she wasn't old enough to act like an old maiden aunt. "Having a man in my life would just be another person to take care of."

Tilly laughed. "I didn't say you needed a husband, or even a boyfriend. You just need to get laid once in a while."

It was Rachel's turn to laugh. "It's been this long, what's the rush?" She swallowed a groan when Tilly's eyes widened. She shouldn't have said anything.

"How long has it been, exactly?"

"Uh–" Rachel waved her hand in the air. That wasn't anybody's business, either. Especially since she'd perfected the art of giving interested men the cold shoulder.

"Knowing you, you haven't gotten any since Anna was conceived, right?" Tilly sounded appalled. "Do you even know how babies are made?"

Rachel pretended to laugh but she could feel her face heating. It was positively old-fashioned these days to save oneself for the man you loved. It was especially odd to someone like Tilly, who treated sleeping around as a pastime, but Rachel had already met the love of her life, and no one she'd met since measured up. "It's been awhile." She took a slow breath to relieve her embarrassment and continued in a light, teasing voice, "So, you see, it's possible to live without sex."

Tilly frowned, taking her situation very seriously. "Well, you shouldn't. Sex is a necessity. It's like food, water, and air. You need it to survive." She paused and looked her friend up and down, assessing. "I'm sure I could find you someone."

"Ah, no thanks, Tilly. I'm good. Really." Tilly's version of a date left a lot to be desired. She could hardly imagine what kind of man Tilly would dredge up for her. Besides that, their manager, Carl, had claimed dibs on her the first time he saw her and he would positively be apoplectic if she started dating.

"No. Listen." Tilly leaned forward and lowered her voice so that none of the patrons at the bar could overhear them. "Anna's already gone for the summer, right?"

Rachel looked at the counter and tried to force down the sick feeling she got in her stomach every time she thought of her nine-year-old daughter spending the whole summer in Florida without her. "She left yesterday morning." And already her heart was breaking.

"Perfect! You can work Big Jim's dinner with me tonight." Rachel was already shaking her head, but Tilly rushed on. "No, you should. The tips are good." She wiggled her perfect eyebrows. "If you play your cards right the tips are *real* good."

"I'm sure the money's great, but the company leaves a lot to be desired."

Tilly waved a hand. "Your standards are awfully high considering you haven't done it in ten years."

Rachel almost laughed. "I haven't slept with a man in ten years *because* my standards are high. Tilly, these guys are drug dealers. You can't deny it."

"They prefer to think of themselves as businessmen. Some of them are really good-looking businessmen."

"Yeah, no thanks. I think I'd rather wait around for Mr. Average-Looking-Stable Man."

Tilly rolled her eyes. "And that's exactly what you'll get – Mr. Boring."

"Life's not all about excitement, Tilly."

"True. But a little more now and then is great, right?" She threw a smile over her shoulder and carried a couple of beers to the group at table twelve.

Rachel watched Tilly deliver the drinks and move on to flirt with the guys at table fifteen. She reminded herself that relationships of any sort were exactly what she'd spent her life trying to avoid. She thought again about Anna. Her daughter was her greatest blessing. Anna was bright and beautiful, and filled with so much curiosity. Rachel treasured her beyond anything she could imagine. But there were also days, really hard lonely days, where she considered the irony of Anna's conception. Somewhere out there was a good man, who'd hopefully gone on to do something important with his life, something to make her sacrifice worthwhile. On those hard days, that hope encouraged her.

It was becoming much more difficult to keep up with Anna's ever-growing interests. Rachel knew she shouldn't turn her back on opportunities for extra tips. Heaven knew they always needed the money, but never at the price she would have to pay. She and Anna might not have as much as they wanted, but she made sure they always had what they needed.

Rachel wasn't a dummy, she knew what went on behind the closed doors of her employer's private dining room. Lately, Big Jim's dinners had become more frequent and more intense. Out of concern for the bar's future she'd even inquired at Wolf Creek's only other restaurant about a waitressing job, but Bailey's Restaurant didn't have any openings. She was thankful that Suds still catered to families and local patrons during the day and early evening hours until the bar opened to a wilder crowd. It was her regulars that still made her job tolerable. She left as many night shifts as she could, and all the special dinners to Tilly.

Special Agent Mike Renner settled into his first-class seat as other passengers filed past, craning their necks to locate seats and stow their carry-ons.

"Catch the hockey game this weekend?" His partner, Gary, was on the phone. Mike pulled a notebook out of his backpack and kicked the pack under his seat. They'd just closed a long undercover case and were each taking a week of downtime before they took on new assignments.

"That center is an ass. How does a guy who skates that badly end up on a pro team?" Mike plopped the book onto the empty seat next to him and muttered, "He ought to switch to golf."

Gary guffawed. "You could have done better,

right?"

Mike acknowledged that with a nod that Gary couldn't see. "Even after all these years, I could out-skate that joke of a player. Listen, it's wheels up in five. I'll call you in a few days."

"Gonna tell Pam and me all about your mystery trip?"

Mike grinned into the phone. "It's just killing you, isn't it? There's nothing to tell. I'm just doing a favor for an old college roommate."

Gary made an exasperated sound over the phone. He knew Mike too well. "Okay, well, try to have a vacation, too. You can't work all the time."

Mike could, and he did. "Talk to you later. Say hi to Pamela for me." He clicked off his phone before Gary could wheedle him any longer. He sent a quick text to let his friend Daniel know he was on his way and then turned his phone off and settled in for the rest of the flight.

Mike picked up the notebook and reviewed his notes again. 'Big Jim' Charles was the suspected kingpin of a drug ring operating out of the tiny town of Wolf Creek, New Hampshire. The town's local police chief had worked closely with Mike's friend, Daniel, when drugs were first found in town, and more recently an informant, but now that the informant had disappeared, Mike agreed with Daniel that it might be time to involve the DEA. He planned to use his downtime to do a little preliminary investigating before taking the case back to his team.

Three hours later, Mike stepped into the dim light of Wolf Creek's only bar, the Suds N Grub, and oriented himself with the floor plan and the customers. The bar was quiet on a Tuesday afternoon; it looked like only locals and they were seated sporadically so as to give each group a measure of privacy.

He helped himself to a table in the front corner near the bar where he had a clear view of the entrance. The dining area was clean if slightly outdated. Despite the fact that he was there to identify drug activity, Mike was really looking forward to a burger and a beer and catching up with his old college roommate.

Daniel arrived right behind him. They exchanged a quick back slap and took their seats.

"Are you going to be recognized?" Mike asked Daniel in a low voice.

Daniel looked around and checked the time on his phone. "Not at this time of day. The troublemakers only come out after happy hour." Daniel looked him over. "You've really let yourself go, Mike." He ribbed with a laugh.

Mike noticed the interested ladies at a nearby table and gave Daniel a shrug. He was a little more muscular, had gotten a few tattoos and an attitude to match over the last several years. In college he'd been as straitlaced as they came, Hockey star, pre-Law.

Mike held out an arm to show off his latest art. "Only henna this time. Just came off a case."

"Nice. I bet that really brings in the ladies."

Mike acknowledged that with a solemn nod. "Not exactly the kind I'm interested in, though. The women I meet are toxic. Beautiful on the outside, corrupt and immoral on the inside."

"You're too young to be so cynical."

"Not when you've seen what I have." Mike dipped his head and looked at his fingers. "I'm starting to think good girls only exist in the movies."

Daniel laughed. "Well, you've come to the right place then. Wolf Creek is a great place to find a good girl."

"Yeah, yours available?"

"Not on your life."

Mike smiled. It was obvious that Daniel was happy. He studied the laminated menu in front of him as the waitress approached to greet them.

"Hey there, what can I bring you guys to drink?" The waitress boldly met his eyes, the invitation plain. "Beer? Or, we have a full bar." She looked him over as she waited for his response.

"Whatever you have on tap is fine with me. And I'll have a burger. Loaded."

Daniel placed his order as well and then braced his

arms on the table. "So how are we going to play this?"

"You're not going to play anything." Mike informed him.

"Come on. I brought this to you. I can help."

Mike frowned at Daniel. "I'm just going to lurk around town for a few days. See what kind of trouble I can find. You can help by finding me a cheap apartment or rental in the bad part of town if we take the case."

"There isn't a good and bad part of Wolf Creek. Everyone here is just getting by. It's more of a slow, comfortable pace. How do you want me to contact you?"

"I've changed your contact in my phone. You can just text me." He leaned in and lowered his voice. "Don't acknowledge me in public after this. I mean it. I don't want you involved in anything I have to do."

Daniel didn't look happy, but he agreed. They spent a quick hour catching up over burgers and beers. Daniel related funny stories about his fiancée, Savannah, and some of the characters in town until Mike held up a hand.

"Don't tell me anymore. I don't want to know more than I should for a new guy." He pulled a sealed envelope from his pocket and handed it over to Daniel. "Do me a favor and give this to your chief of police." His face was serious. "Directly to Bill, don't leave it for him, and don't give it to anyone to give him." He tapped the envelope with his forefinger. "These are my credentials and a way to contact me or my team. It's better if I'm not seen talking to him until we have a legitimate reason to meet." He took a swig from his beer. "So, how do I go about getting myself arrested around here?"

"You haven't changed a bit." Daniel lied. They both laughed.

Chapter 2

It turned out to be surprisingly easy to get himself picked up by the police. Mike suspected that Chief Bill Mobely had been watching for him to make a move, and though Mike was afraid it would look obvious, he couldn't blame the chief. The faster the Wolf Creek Police Department could get a DEA investigation underway, the faster they could see results.

Mike waited in the stark cell for the chief to make his way back to the holding area to question him. To support his cover, Mike slouched against the wall and stared insolently at the deputies on desk duty. The way they regarded him confirmed he'd pulled it off.

No more than an hour passed before the chief ambled into view, unlocked the cell, and beckoned Mike forward. No words were exchanged as he was ushered into a stuffy, windowless interview room. The door closed with a heavy click.

The chief seated himself across a Formica-topped table and stacked his hands in front of him. Feeling no need for pretense now, Mike sat across from him and leaned forward, ready to get to work.

"Mike Renner, I presume?" The chief reached out to shake his hand.

"Good to meet you, sir."

"I took the liberty of pulling your record. I'm impressed. We sure got lucky to have you looking into our little situation out here."

Mike inclined his head. "Daniel Harrison is a good friend. I can't promise the DEA will take your case, but I'm here to see what you're up against and I'll take it back to my team."

Bill sat back, looking pleased. "Well, that's more than we've got now so we'll take it. I'll be the first to admit that this situation is over my head. Around here, we don't get much more than a little B & E and some domestic calls. This drug problem is tricky, and I'm not sure where to start. I can share my suspicions with you, but so far I haven't been able to act on any of it, especially now that our informant is MIA." He dipped his chin. "This is a small town, and I have to live in it when the fire burns to embers."

Mike nodded his understanding. He knew how difficult it was to expose a secret that large and keep the peace at the same time. It certainly wasn't a one-man operation. "I'm here to see if I can help."

Bill smacked his hands together and then pulled a file from the back of the yellow legal pad he'd carried in with him. "Let's get down to business." He slid the file across the desk. Mike flipped through it as he listened to Bill lay out his suspicions.

"I know Jim Charles and his minions are organizing some kind of meetings in that back room at the bar, but without my informant, I can't place anyone in there. My force isn't experienced enough with surveillance and this town's too damn small to put someone undercover. Also, Suds is a family establishment during the day, as far as I can tell it's still a legitimate business. I can't just call in the troops. I'm sure you understand that a sting could only work if we picked 'em all up at the same time. We'd never get another shot at this."

"You'd have a better chance at a sting by bringing in strangers, people that might look like tourists."

Bill snorted. "We don't get a lot of tourists. Newcomers would make then suspicious."

Mike thought of another angle. "Maybe not. Maybe what they need is a little healthy competition."

Bill eyed him. "You're not gonna distribute, are you? Because I can't get behind that."

"It's not my preferred approach, but if I do I'll bring in someone I trust. I agree, it's time to cut off the locals."

"Well, I'll trust your judgment. How soon could you set something up?"

"I'd like to hang around for a while, get an idea of what we're up against. Get a feel for the players, the game, their schedules."

"Coupla weeks?"

Mike nodded. "At least. I'll need to hang around, let them get to know me."

"Need us to leave you alone?"

Mike considered that. "Not necessary. It would be helpful if your force doesn't follow me around, but otherwise, treat me like you would any other suspicious newcomer." An hour later, they shook hands and parted, Mike leaving with the same bad attitude he had when he arrived. Damn, but he like the chief of police.

For the next few days, Mike hung around Suds N Grub at various times but mostly after the dinner crowd had thinned, watching the manager, Carl, hit on patrons, female staff, it didn't seem to matter. He was lecherous to every single female between eighteen and fifty.

Mike made his presence known using his own tried and true methods, chatting up the same women. He made note of the pattern of customers coming and going. It didn't take long to identify the players and by the end of the week he was confident he had a case to bring back to the DEA.

Before heading back to D.C., Mike made the short trip out to see Daniel. His friend was living on the grounds of an old manor on the border between Wolf Creek and the Maliut Indian Nation, that his fiancée, Savannah, was turning into a museum to highlight the history of the local tribe.

The drive was scenic, along a quiet tree lined, two lane highway. The road curved and dipped, teasing him with glimpses of deep green hills and valleys off in the distance. He turned off onto a nearly hidden gravel path as Daniel had instructed and followed it around behind the majestic brick building to a smaller cabin off to the side. Daniel greeted him at the door.

"Hey. Come on in." He held the door for Mike to precede him and then followed him into the enormous open living room.

Mike looked around. "This is nice."

"Thanks. We're comfortable here. And, it's close to the museum so Savannah can keep an eye on things." Daniel paused to laugh. "She's a little protective of the place."

Mike watched Daniel sit on one of the couches and throw an arm over the back. Even though he hadn't yet met Savannah, he found himself a little jealous of Daniel. His friend had found a place to call home and he was clearly happy. There were so many times, like this one, when Mike wished he could settle down somewhere and leave the travel and the duplicity of the job behind him. His lifestyle had been exciting when he was younger, but after nearly a decade in the field, he was burned out.

He leaned forward, getting down to business. "There's definitely a case here. I'm heading back to

D.C. in a few hours, but I'm going to run this by my team and see how quickly we can get things rolling. It should be a slam dunk because the guys around here aren't even being careful." He paused to shake his head, looking incredulous. "They must think they're gods, or something."

Daniel gave a nod. "That about sums up Jim Charles. When you own half the town and look like Santa Clause, people aren't terribly motivated to turn you in."

"If I can get the support, I'm hoping to be back here in another week or so. I'm not going to need much of a cover since they don't appear to be a very sophisticated operation. I'll give you a call when I have the details."

"Sounds good. When this is all over you need to stay on for a while. I'd love for you to get to know Savannah."

"That would be nice."

Six hours later Mike was back in his townhouse. After seeing how comfortably his friend lived, he looked around with a new eye. By D.C. standards the place was nice. But it wasn't home. The furnishings were expensive and well matched, but apart from a few items he'd gotten from his parents over the years and his cat who now spent most of its time being looked after by an elderly neighbor, the place had no personality. He thought about Daniel, how he'd recently left a great job with Rutgers University in New

Jersey to move to New Hampshire to be close to the woman he loved, and he found himself wishing his own life was that simple. Or maybe just wishing he could meet a woman that was genuine and had a good heart. Or, maybe he just needed to get laid.

Chapter 3

Rachel gulped a few ounces of coffee and threw a change of clothes into a tote bag. After church she hoped to work with Savannah at the museum. One of the Maliut elders had recently acquired a few boxes of new artifacts and she knew that Savannah was anxious to dig in.

Typically, Sunday was Rachel's only day off because the bar was closed. Besides catching up on housework, she liked to do something special with Anna. Funds were always tight, so they limited their activities to going to Bailey's Restaurant for dessert or renting a movie and making popcorn. Whatever they chose, it was a special time that they set aside each week. Now that Anna was in Florida for nearly the whole summer, Rachel found the quiet lonely and unsettling. She gave Savannah a call on her way to church.

"I'm free this afternoon if you could use my help with those new boxes."

"Oh Rachel, that would be awesome. There's so much here to examine." She was quiet for a moment.

"It's Sunday. Are you sure you don't want the time for yourself today?"

Rachel tried for a laugh but it fell flat over the phone so she decided to be honest. "I don't want to be alone today."

"Ah, gotcha." Savannah cleared her throat. "Well, lucky for you I need a lot of help. Come on over when you're ready and I'll get you started sorting things."

"Thanks. I'll see you soon."

Rachel normally treated the Sunday church service as her weekly injection of good to counteract the fact that her primary job was waitressing in a bar. Today's service though focused on the passing of a young man on the reservation whose death came as the result of driving while under the influence of drugs. As the pastor talked about temptation and the result of poor decisions, prayed for his family, and for the soul of yet another young man that was gone too soon, Rachel thought about the escalating problem in their quiet little town. She strongly suspected her employer was the man to blame for introducing a booming new industry to Wolf Creek, but at the same time without the paycheck the bar provided she'd never be able to keep herself and Anna above water. The tips were generous enough, even without resorting to Tilly's extra-curricular activities and mostly he respected her determination to remain on the more respectable side of his business dealings. One day, she hoped to go back to school and finish her degree, but for now Anna was her sole focus. Rachel silently added a prayer for an end to the danger and depravity worming its way into their little town.

After the service she gave a friendly nod to the ladies that often invited her to stay for coffee and made a bee-line for her car to make the trip across town to the former Alder Manor where the new Maliut Indian museum had recently been established.

Rachel found Savannah in one of the rooms off the main hall they'd designated as a prep room. Typical of her unconventional friend, she was sitting cross-legged on the floor, boxes stacked around her. She looked like a child at Christmas, surveying a stack of gifts. Rachel looked around in wonder too. "Where did they find all this?"

Savannah shrugged and turned bright eyes on Rachel. It was clear she had a great deal of passion for her job. "I suspect someone was holding onto it until they knew whether or not they could trust me."

Rachel silently agreed. Savannah'd had a hard time convincing the tribe that her motives were true and the Tribe's mistrust of the Wolf Creek residents ran generations deep. The rift was healing bit by bit, but it was a tender truce, and the new drug trade was already straining those tiny strides. Rachel peeked into a few of the boxes. "This is amazing stuff. I'm really glad they've entrusted it to you."

"So am I," Savannah mumbled. She was already focused on the box in front of her.

Rachel got right to work photographing the items and organizing them for Savannah to begin her research. They'd been working together for only a few months, but already they had a well-choreographed routine and the process went fast. They worked until mid-afternoon when Daniel showed up with drinks and sandwiches for them both.

As he passed out the food, Daniel asked Savannah, "Have you told Rachel the news?"

Savannah shook her head and swallowed the bite she'd just taken. She looked over at Rachel with a glow in her eyes. "We've decided to hold the wedding reception here."

Rachel laughed. "Well, I kind of expected that." She turned to Daniel in a falsetto voice making them both laugh. "Not like she's obsessed with the place or anything."

"We're thinking the end of September, and we'd like you and Anna to be in the wedding party."

Tears sprang to Rachel's eyes. It was sweet the way they'd taken her and Anna into their lives. She appreciated not just their friendship and support, but the way they never judged her or asked uncomfortable questions about how she's come to be a single parent. They accepted her for who she was now, and that was more than she'd experienced anywhere before moving to Wolf Creek.

"We'd love to! Anna will be over the moon about

this."

"I want to keep things small, so it'll just be you, my sister, and Daniel's sister, and then Anna and Daniel's niece as junior bridesmaids. For the guys, my brother, Daniel's brother-in-law, and his friend Mike if he can get the time off. His nephew will be a junior groomsman." Savannah turned loving eyes on Daniel and he returned her look with one of his own. Rachel swallowed the painful swoop of yearning and gave what she hoped was an adequate smile.

Mike dialed his dad as he carried his bags into the rental house Daniel had arranged for him. It was nicer than he expected as usually his undercover situations brought him to hovels. This house was a three-bedroom ranch with two baths and a decent yard. It was made for a family. In that case, it was wasted on him, but he appreciated Daniel's thoughtfulness.

"Mike! How was your flight?"

Mike spoke to his father several times a week. Despite the distance and Mike's crazy life, they remained close. Mike's mother had passed away just over a year earlier from breast cancer, leaving Mike and Gray with only each other to hold together their little family.

"Short. It's only an hour and a half. Not a bad commute."

"What do you think of the town? Nice place?"

"It's your typical small town. The businesses have funny names. There's a flower shop called Fresh Cuts, and the beauty shop is the Silver Salon." He paused to chuckle. "The local coffee shop is Beans and Bagels."

"Sounds quaint."

"Quaint, with an undercurrent of evil."

"Right up your alley, then." His dad chuckled.

"I guess so. It will be good to see Daniel again, though."

"Wasn't he a professor of Criminology at Rutgers, or something? How'd he end up in New Hampshire?"

Mike stowed his duffel under the bed and headed to the kitchen to see what he needed to pick up from the store. "He was up here for research and met someone."

"Ah, yes. Love."

"Must be. I haven't met her yet. She must be something, for him to move three states away just to be with her."

"Love does that to a man. You'll see someday."

Mike grunted. "I'll take your word for it." He knew his father was ready for him to settle down, too. "It's not likely to happen anytime soon. Not even a good idea in my line of work. Who wants a husband who's away all the time? Besides, the women I come in contact with hardly count as the marry-em-and-settle-down type, ya know?"

"I know, son. But still, I have hope."

"That makes one of us."

Mike's next stop was Suds N Grub for dinner and to shake things up a bit. He was greeted by a blast of air conditioning providing welcome relief from the humidity that hung in the air outside. He cased the scene and selected his favorite table near the bar. There were a few open seats at the bar but that wouldn't have suited his purpose. His goal was to engage the attention of a certain tall blond and stacked waitress.

Confident in his ability to draw any woman's attention, Mike had dressed his part in a black t-shirt just tight enough to accentuate his sculpted biceps and worn jeans that rode low on his hips. He donned a battered baseball cap pulled low to shield his eyes.

Taking a seat, Mike leaned back in his chair and rested a tattooed forearm casually on the table in front of him. He stared at the waitress's back and waited. It didn't take long for her to sense his attention. She turned and met his gaze unerringly, sauntering toward him with a confidence that would be sexy if he was interested in that sort of woman.

"Hey, I'm Tilly. What can I get 'cha?"

Mike lowered his eyelids and appraised her boldly before speaking. She was hot, there was no denying it. But her kind of eagerness turned him off. "A tall one. You know where I can get, ah, party supplies, around here?"

Tilly didn't even blink. "You came to the right place because I can hook you up. Let me go grab that beer."

He watched as she sashayed up to the bar and poured him a tall draft. She whispered to the bartender and then returned with the glass. She reached across him slowly to set it down, brushing a good deal of her chest against his shoulder. He resisted the urge to lean away.

"Carl's gonna come out and talk to ya in a few minutes. He's the guy to know for just about anything around here." She leaned a hip against the table next to his arm. "You busy later? I get off around one. You could too." She winked.

Mike tipped his head and laughed. "Don't know yet. But if I'm around, I'll come find you."

Tilly raised an eyebrow. "I'll be counting on it." She slid a slip of paper in front of him with her number on it. He tucked it in his pocket and took a long swig of his drink as he watched Tilly bounce off to flirt with the men at another table.

Carl left him waiting ten more minutes but Mike wasn't surprised. He'd dealt with the type before. Controlling the circumstance was how Carl wielded power. Mike appraised the man as Carl entered the dining room from a back room and headed toward Mike's table. Carl was tall and bulky, but not particularly muscular. He'd probably been good looking at one time but recent years had made him soft.

He walked with confidence that told Mike he could still hold his own in a fight.

"Carl Williams," the man announced as he pulled out a chair and sat across from Mike.

"Mike Black."

"Black, huh?" Carl studied him. "Not a lot of Blacks around here."

"I'm not from around here."

"Where ya from, then?"

"Here and there. We getting personal?" Mike intentionally took the offensive, laying his attitude on thick.

"Just makin' conversation. Tilly says you're looking for supplies."

"Yep."

"What kind of supplies you talkin' about? Pot? Coke?"

Mike gave him a look of disdain. "That's baby shit. I'm looking for wholesale. Real stuff. Blow, hardball, red bullets, acid, Big H. High end stuff. I'm told this shithole of a town has a supplier. I'll give you a finders fee to get me in."

Carl was silent for a long time. "Where's your market?"

Mike gave him a knowing smile. "Here and there.

We don't share a market, if that's your concern. I've got my own. My own distribution, too. My last supplier went dry."

Carl turned his head and ticked a finger at Tilly, who immediately brought him a drink, whiskey by the look of it. He sipped it before looking up at Mike again. "Might take a few days. How long you in town for?"

"As long as I need to be."

Carl frowned. "Are you familiar with our product?"

"It'll do."

"How do you transport?"

"Customized car for small loads. Do you have enough supply for a larger transport?"

Carl leaned forward and practically rubbed his hands together. Mike could see the wheels turning in his head. "We can get it."

"Local?"

"No. Heck, no. We import. And we can get real high-end stuff. China girl and caps, even way up here. There's more of a market than you'd expect in this backwoods area."

Mike sat back and picked up his beer. Hard drugs were being imported to Wolf Creek. Maybe this was a bigger operation than he thought. "I'm impressed."

Carl gave a satisfied smile. "We run a tight ship

and we control the region. It brings a lot of capital."

Mike doubted the quality of the operation, but he kept those thoughts to himself as he listened to Carl describe the operation, giving away more than a seasoned player would have. At the rate Carl was dumping information Mike would have the sting set and cinched inside a week.

As soon as Carl wound down Mike set up plans to meet with Big Jim. They agreed on a time and place a week out to meet up again. Mike finished off his beer and pulled out his wallet to drop a bill on the table but Carl interrupted. "On the house, buddy."

Mike didn't wait around for Tilly's shift to be over. In truth, he just wasn't that desperate. Instead, he returned to his rental house and logged into the government's secure server. He emailed a report to his team and requested a wire transfer for the cash he'd need to convince Big Jim that Mike's operation was solid. He was confident that with a few weeks of surveillance and a little luck, this would be case closed.

A week later Mike was back at Suds N Grub to have dinner with the self-esteemed head of Wolf Creek's drug ring, Big Jim Charles. Judging by Carl's unguarded and somewhat showy attitude, he could guess that Carl had been impressed by his façade and had spoken to Big Jim about him.

Mike was early so he took a seat at the bar, ordered

a drink, and swiveled around to watch the crowd of diners and drinkers. Tilly wasn't on duty tonight. Tonight's waitress was taller, thinner, and moved with an innate gracefulness that appealed to Mike. She was older than Tilly, probably around thirty, and not bad looking, but had the appearance of a woman that was worn out by life. She approached the bar to retrieve a drink order and Mike took a harder look at her. She barely spared him a glance as she took the loaded tray and headed back into the dining room. It was her dismissive look that snapped her into place in his memory. "Shit." Though there was a decade and nearly forty states between here and college, Mike was certain she was the woman he'd nearly turned himself inside out over all those years ago. A woman he thought he'd loved. "Rachel Henige," he muttered to himself. "Freaking great."

They'd been lab partners in college, and from the first day of that class, Mike had been hooked on her. She hadn't shown the least interest in him at first but he'd spent nearly seven weeks of class convincing her that he was worth her attention. By the end of the semester they'd become friends. They'd spent one amazingly perfect weekend together studying for finals, where friendship turned into more, and more lovemaking took place than actual studying. They'd dated a few more times after that and then, when they separated for semester break she disappeared and he hadn't heard from her again. She was a barely healed scar on his memory, and here she was. He was certain of it.

Catching the bartender's attention, Mike leaned close. "That waitress, what's her name?"

"Ice Queen?" The bartender shook his head. "You're probably looking for Tilly."

Mike blinked at the man. "This one's not like Tilly?"

The other man gave a short dry laugh. "No. Rachel is nothing like Tilly."

Mike turned around and leaned his forearms against the bar, dropping his chin down nearly to his chest as he evaluated the situation. It was Rachel. Shit. Would she remember him? If she did, would she blow his cover? He pulled his baseball cap down low and turned back to face her while he thought about his next move.

Mike watched Rachel from his corner spot and noted several things. Her mannerisms hadn't changed much over the years. She still held herself with the same dignity that had drawn him to her the first time. Second, she seemed to be well-liked by the patrons. In direct contrast to Tilly, she didn't flirt or act outrageous in any way, instead she worked hard with a quiet and capable grace.

He swirled his whiskey but he didn't take a drink. In truth, he hated whiskey. It was nothing more than a prop for his disguise and fussing with his glass gave him something to do with his hands. He'd been mentally prepared for this first meeting with Big Jim but now he was distracted. He wished he could reschedule tonight's meeting to give himself more time to think though how Rachel's presence could change things.

He couldn't pull his eyes away as Rachel bent to place a tray on a neighboring table. Her tiny rear end was close enough that his fingers actually itched to reach out and touch it. It was as if time had fallen away and he was right back in college, admiring and wanting her. Where Rachel was concerned, he'd never had any control.

Mike glared at his drink and lifted his glass to pretend to down another gulp when he realized there was a new angle to consider. Could she be involved in the drug trade? He watched as Carl sidled up to Rachel and spoke to her in a low voice. Whatever he was saying didn't appear to sit well with her because Mike could see her face darkening as she listened. Carl placed a heavy arm around her shoulder as he leaned into her, crowding her against the bar top. His beefy arm made its way down her back until it curved around her abdomen, his fingers reaching just under her breast. Mike saw Rachel try to step away but Carl increased his pressure and hauled her back into his side.

Mike's stomach turned sour at the look of revulsion on Rachel's face. He never liked to see women manhandled, but with Rachel it stronger than that. He released a pent-up breath. As much as he wanted to, he couldn't intervene without tipping his hand. The best he could do was create a minor distraction and hope like hell she played along.

He dropped his glass between their feet. Rachel sprang back to avoid the splash and Carl glowered at him.

"Sorry." Mike squatted to take the glass from Rachel, who'd automatically bent to retrieve it. While near the floor their eyes met. He looked up at Carl as he hooked an arm around Rachel's elbow and helped her to her feet. "Splashed a little on your shoes, man."

Carl lifted a whiskey splattered foot to inspect the leather and stalked off toward the restaurant's office with a ferocious expression on his face.

Rachel's eyes locked on his face and she flushed a deep red before going pale. For a moment he continued to hold her elbow, concerned she might pass out. Her gaze slide away from Mike's face, something like humiliation replaced her shocked expression. "Thanks." Her voice was quiet, but he'd recognize it anywhere. "I–I need to go."

Mike nodded with an intentionally distracted look and turned back to the bar, not giving witnesses a reason to read anything into the moment.

Rachel turned and fairly ran back to the kitchen to call Savannah. She knew the call could have waited until her break but she used it as an excuse to gain a few minutes of peace to calm her racing heart. When Savannah picked up on the second ring, Rachel knew she must have been near the phone.

"I am so sorry, Savannah. Tilly didn't show up for her shift so Carl needs me to work a double shift tonight. I'm not going to be able to help you with those boxes after all."

"Where's Tilly?" Savannah wondered.

"I don't know, but she owes me big for this! Now I'm working a double shift today, and I have to work again tomorrow afternoon."

"It's okay. I've got everything under control here. Ski brought up a few kids from the reservation and they'll help me get everything moved."

"Oh, Savannah." Rachel sighed in exasperation. "Don't work on the new exhibits tonight. Sit down and put your feet up. I'll be there tomorrow after my shift."

"We'll see. Take care, Rachel."

Rachel hung up the phone and leaned her forehead against the cool block wall. Her heart was pounded so hard she thought it might just explode. Mike Renner was in her restaurant. What was he doing here? Had he recognized her? She couldn't tell. She reached up to smooth her hair and then let her hand drop in disgust. She was a waitress in a bar in a middle-of-nowhere town and he'd just seen her being felt up by her manager. No, if he'd recognized her, he surely would be thanking his lucky stars that he'd gotten away from her so many years ago. She tried to suck in a breath but couldn't get enough air. For just a brief moment she started to panic. Should she run? No, she couldn't run when Anna was away, having the time of her life with her best friend in Florida. It wouldn't be fair. And besides, Rachel had dealt with harder things. This was her home and she would stay. He probably hadn't even recognized her. She was safe. She drew a slow, steady breath and then another.

Just a few more hours. Then she could go home. Alone. After Jim's dinner a lonely bed would feel like heaven. She grabbed a clean white apron from a hook in the corner of the enormous stainless kitchen.

She shook her head. Running into Mike was just a coincidence. Random encounters could happen. People wrote books about it all the time. She pushed her turbulent thoughts aside and steadied herself to sneak into the private dining room in the back of the restaurant where she would hover near the door until Jim finished his opening comments.

" … can't trust the foreign markets … can't trust outsiders to get the product out …" He could have been talking about anything from exports to investments. She pressed her lips together to keep herself from reacting to Jim's words. The less attention she drew to herself, the better.

She distracted herself by studying each of the men sitting around the large table. After waiting tables for nearly ten years, she could usually predict which hands she would be dodging by the third round of drinks. Tonight's guests include a few locals, a couple of men she didn't recognize, along with Carl and his buddy, Paul. For the most part, they were Jim's usual mix of the adventurous and the desperate. Her gaze landed stopped short on Mike and her stomach dropped. He was into drugs? From the corner of the room she allowed herself to study him. His face hadn't changed. Even after all these years, she'd know it anywhere. He was larger now, his body filled out like a man in his prime instead of the lanky young man she'd known so well. His T-shirt partially concealed a tattoo on his inner arm and showed off a couple of tribal tats on his forearms. He was different but no less sexy. Her reaction to him didn't surprise her, though. She knew that no matter how far he'd fallen, she'd always feel the same about him.

He chatted easily with one of the guys from Black River but she felt his eyes on her as she made her way around the table taking drink orders. She paused when she heard him introduce himself as Mike Black in a voice so very familiar that it made her trip. She was relieved when he turned his attention back to Jim while she served them food. Seated at the head of the table like a king, Jim's look and attitude were every bit as pompous, and she found herself embarrassed to be seen working in such conditions. With his snow-white beard and big booming laugh, she knew most people in town saw him as a jovial benefactor, but here in this setting, Rachel only saw him as the criminal he was, worse somehow for his duplicity.

As the next hours wore on, she noted that Mike

had quietly switched to flat ginger ale as the other guys kept drinking and enjoying themselves at Big Jim's expense. Their stories got bigger, their laughter got louder, and their hands got freer. She fended off subtle and not-so-subtle advances from the men she was serving. She dodged the hands that landed on her behind or at the hem of her black skirt and she held her expression as inappropriate comments were directed her way.

One of the men hitched a finger in the waistband of her skirt and tugged her into his side with a wicked gleam in his eye that he probably thought was sexy. "I'm in need of a little dessert, sweetheart. What do you have on offer?"

Rachel took a step back and to her relief, Carl spoke up with his usual mix of jealousy and disgust for her. "Hey now. That's the Ice Queen. She's not on the menu. If she were into men, I'd have had her years ago." Carl laughed and most of the men joined in, adding comments of their own. Mike didn't join in but she knew he watched her for a reaction. Her eyes burned and she felt sick. Normally she appreciated Carl's attitude. She'd been putting him off for years and that only served to further protect her from men like the ones around the table tonight, but this time she wanted to melt in shame. What did he think of her now?

It was well after two a.m. when the party finally

broke up. Mike was exhausted, and Rachel looked to be dead on her feet. As Carl was leading a few of the guests to the parking lot, Mike finally took his chance to speak to her. "Can I give you a lift?"

"Thank you. No. I don't live far."

He squinted at her. "Are any of these idiots likely to follow you home?"

A little smile. "I'll be fine."

He reassured himself that she'd be okay, that she'd probably been doing this for years, but his protective nature urged him to follow her home anyway. He knew it was too risky. He needed time to think things through. Now that he'd made his way into Jim's inner circle, he couldn't risk the chance she'd remember him and blow his cover, so he squeezed her elbow and left before his conscience caused him to change his mind.

Mike sent his notes off to his team as soon as he got home and then dropped into bed. He was exhausted but he had a feeling sleep wouldn't come. His mind was spinning with questions. What was Rachel Henige doing waiting tables in a seedy bar and restaurant in Wolf Creek, New Hampshire? When he'd last seen her, she'd been the star of the university dive team and a brilliant med student. What forced her life so far off track?

She had to have followed a man here, he reasoned with a sick knot in the pit of his stomach. Why else would a woman like her end up waiting tables two thousand miles from where she grew up? He let himself think back to college. The chemistry between them was off the charts right from the beginning, but their friendship, the closeness he felt with her had been truly rare and special. Of course he wondered and worried when she didn't come back the next semester, but he'd assumed it was money trouble or family issues that kept her away. Hell, he'd even considered that something horrible had happened to her. He'd never one considered that she'd left to be with another man. He'd been her first lover, her only lover when they'd been together so the idea that she could have left him so suddenly for someone else made him feel ill.

He rolled onto his side and punched his pillow into shape. His mind kept bringing him back to her reactions at dinner as the men tried copping a feel, or even just flirting with her. She didn't enjoy their attention and Carl's hint that she might be gay seemed to throw her for a loop as well. He gritted his teeth as he thought about the way Big Jim he watched over the proceedings as she was entertainment. That graceful, beautiful woman had been treated like property.

Having dealt with some pretty depraved individuals over the years, he was well aware that it was often circumstances that held people captive in their roles. What were Rachel's circumstances? If she knew who he was, would she keep his secret?

He refocused his thoughts on whether she would be a help or a hindrance to his case. She was well positioned to give him news and gossip that he would depend on to gather evidence for a strong case against Jim Charles. If she knew who he was, would she be willing to play along? On the other hand, if she was here because she had followed a man across the country, no matter what his gut told him about her nature, her loyalty could still lie on the wrong side of the law. In that case, revealing himself could be a really bad thing. He flopped onto his back and stacked his hands behind his head. There was so much to consider.

Two miles across town, Rachel stepped into a hot shower and leaned against the wall. What sick twist of fate could possibly have brought Mike Renner here? She'd been curious about him over the years and had even tried looking him up online, but not much ever came up about him. As silly as it was, she still missed him. She missed the special bond they'd had. She liked to imagine that the reason he was invisible online was because he had some clandestine job with the government, though she knew that was pretty far-fetched.

Was it possible that he'd tracked her here? No. She was a nobody. He may have looked for her right after her disappearance, but there was no way he'd still be thinking about her after all these years. And besides, she reasoned, she'd never told anyone where she was from, not even Buzzy, who'd been the first person she met when she arrived in Wolf Creek, or June who'd taken her in and gotten her a job. Maybe her parents had been looking for her. No! She wouldn't go there.

She'd made the right decision for herself at the time, and she'd never allowed room for what-ifs. Mike hadn't given her any real indication tonight that he knew who she was, and if he did somehow remember her, she'd just have to roll with it. She was who she was.

She closed her eyes and let the hot water spill over her. He still looked good, if a little tougher than she remembered. His black hair, and those dark eyes! Even now, remembering how he'd made her laugh, how he touched her and made her feel beautiful, stirred her heart. How was he involved with the cretins that had Wolf Creek in a stranglehold? She shook her head even though no one was there to see it. No, she couldn't believe he'd have fallen so far. But then again, he'd had an easy life, his father a doctor. Maybe those things had lured him into a wasted life. Her stomach tumbled and her limbs went heavy with the impact of that idea. She finished her shower and went to bed with images of what might have set Mike on his current path playing out in her mind.

Rachel woke the next morning feeling wrung out, and a quick glance in the mirror as she made her way to the kitchen confirmed she looked as bad as she felt. She paused to knock on Anna's door before remembering that Anna was in Florida. The sick feeling in her gut returned. She didn't even have Anna to distract her. Of course, that was probably for the best right now. Her own little world had been knocked sideways last night, and as perceptive as Anna was, she knew her daughter would notice.

Chapter 4

Rachel's shift was nearly up when Tilly blew through the next day in a wave of smiles and excuses. Her sudden reappearance didn't matter to Rachel, much. She was used to Tilly's unpredictability and she had to admit that she was thankful Tilly nearly always worked the evening shifts so that Rachel could be home with Anna, and far away from the bar scene.

"Oh my gosh, Rachel. What a night!" Tilly gushed as she stowed her purse and clocked in.

"Everything okay?"

"Great." She tilted her head in question and then brightened. "Oh! No, I mean I had the most amazing night."

"I was worried that something had happened to you. I almost called."

Tilly looked confused so Rachel explained. "You missed your shift last night. Jim's dinner?"

Comprehension dawned on Tilly's beautiful face. "Crap! I am so sorry, Rach."

"It's fine. The tips were good as you said."

Tilly was a good enough friend to know how much Rachel hated working Big Jim's dinners. "Did you have plans?"

"I didn't have anything going that I couldn't reschedule."

Tilly's attention floated across the room as a customer entered and Rachel saw her face light up. Before Rachel could say anything further, Tilly was across the room and had planted herself in a man's lap as he took a seat at a table. Tilly's action wasn't unusual; that wasn't what caught Rachel's attention. No, it was the owner of the lap she occupied. Evidently, Tilly knew Mike.

Rachel spun toward the bar giving them her back when Mike started to lift his head. Her stomach churned with what she recognized as jealousy and she cursed herself. He wasn't hers, and it was better that he didn't recognize her. She decided it would be better to clear out before she was forced to witness any more of Tilly's special brand of flirting. Rachel clenched her teeth and forced her imagination away from the unbidden images of Tilly and Mike together under more graphic circumstances.

Rachel clocked out with a relieved sigh. She was so tired she could hardly move. She'd worked Tilly's shift until late last night then laid awake wondering what Mike was doing in Wolf Creek. Her alarm went off before she'd even fallen asleep and she'd worked another eight hour shift.

"Got a plate here for you, Rach."

Rachel turned and shot Tiny a grateful smile. The plate he held out to her contained a bar burger and cheese fries. "Something to stick to your ribs."

She nearly swooned but collected herself and leaned in to kiss him on the cheek instead. The old cook had known her nearly as long as she'd been in town, and for the last ten years, he'd been like an uncle to her. "Thank you, Tiny."

"You look like you could use a good meal and a long uninterrupted nap. Well, I can't vouch for the food," he began with a wink, "but I'll put the word out for everyone to leave you alone for a while."

Rachel huffed a quiet laugh. Everyone knew he was the best short order cook in the county. His food was probably the only reason people in Wolf Creek even bothered with Suds N Grub, unless they were there to do business with Carl or Big Jim.

"Take your plate into the dining room and make Tilly wait on you. She owes you one."

Rachel nodded and stifled a yawn. She didn't relish the idea of trying to eat while watching Tilly maul Mike, but she was too tired to come up with an excuse for staying in the kitchen, and she knew Tiny would know something was up if she made a fuss.

She pushed her way through the swinging double

doors and found an empty table for two in the corner between the bar and the kitchen. It would be dark enough to hide, and relatively quiet. She settled into the chair and rested an elbow on the table as she picked at her cheese fries. She wondered if she was too tired to lift her burger.

Doug was the bartender on duty tonight and he caught her eye to see if she needed anything. Rachel loved working with Doug. The man could read her mind. Less than a minute later he was there, plunking a large ice water in front of her. She gave him a weary smile and sipped it from a straw.

Rachel worked her way through half of her fries and a few bites of her burger before Tilly materialized beside her, fanning her face with one manicured hand.

"That man is H-O-T, hot. Oh, my gawd!"

Rachel swallowed around the sudden constriction in her throat. "Yeah? You close the deal yet?" She hated to ask and really didn't want to hear Tilly's answer, but she also knew that Tilly would be disappointed if Rachel didn't ask. So, she acted as if seeing Tilly sitting on Mike's lap didn't nearly send her into a tailspin.

"No. I swear he is playing hard to get." She leaned in and giggled. "It just makes him all the more fun."

Rachel forced a smile.

Tilly cocked her head. "You okay?"

"I'm exhausted. Two eights yesterday back-to-back and here again today."

"Oh, right. Sorry." She shifted her stance and tapped one of her long nails against her lips. "I'll take your next shift, okay? That'll give you," she scrunched up her face thinking, "two days off."

Rachel nodded but didn't look up from her burger. "Thanks. That would be great." With Anna gone she probably would have made better use of her time by working. But two days away from the bar was too good an opportunity to pass up.

Tilly bounced away to wait on other customers. Rachel dropped her chin back into her hand and chanced a look over to where Mike was sitting. He was leaning back in his chair, negligently turning his beer with one hand while the other rested on his thigh. He stared at her with an unreadable expression on his dark face.

Embarrassed, Rachel dropped her gaze back to her unfinished burger. Her stomach twisted and she nudged her plate away. She needed to leave, and fast.

She felt his eyes on her as she picked up her dishes and headed back to the kitchen. Doug smiled as she passed the bar, and she managed a reciprocal smile. The bright lights and clanging sounds of the kitchen were almost a welcome reprieve from Mike's burning gaze. Tiny met her halfway taking the dishes from her.

"Go. Get out of here." He gave her a quick peck

on the forehead. "I want to hear that you slept until at least noon tomorrow, okay?"

Rachel gave a small laugh and a nod. "I'll do my best."

Grabbing her purse she let herself out the back door to walk the three blocks home.

Mike watched the familiar interaction between Rachel and the bartender with approval. The bartender's brotherly attention and concern tracked with the way Mike remembered people reacted to Rachel. There had been something about her that people respected, and somehow that made them want to care for her. Evidently, that much hadn't changed.

When Rachel didn't return after a few minutes, Mike supposed she'd gone home for the night. He would have loved to follow her, to see where she lived, maybe even to speak to her. But tonight he had work to do. Tilly unknowingly played her part perfectly, though he wasn't interested in what she was offering. He was tired of that particular game, tired of the suggestive teasing. In his opinion, a little modesty was infinitely more attractive. Looking at Tilly, he decided that if he ever had a daughter, he'd dress her like a nun until she was thirty. Rachel was still modest, he thought with a smile. Even working at a bar, she covered herself and was nothing but polite to her customers. Regardless of what had brought her here, he was relieved to see that those traits he'd loved so much about her were still there.

Just then Tilly dropped back into his lap. Shifting to allow room between them, Mike turned his focus on her, shuttering his eyes to hide his disinterest.

Tilly leaned in to nuzzle his neck. "Carl has a job for you. If you're interested."

Mike pulled back and gave her a hard look, suspecting that Carl was testing him, maybe even watching them now. "I don't work for Carl. I have my own crew."

If Tilly was bothered by his anger she didn't show it. "This is just a quickie." She slapped at him playfully as if he'd taken the bait. "Not that kind of quickie, though that can be arranged, too." She paused to give him an opening to take her up on her offer. He raised an eyebrow at her, letting her interpret that however she was inclined. After a moment, she sighed and continued, "No reason you can't make a little cash on the side, though, right?" She reached into her stretchy tight top and pulled out a scrap of paper with some details scrawled on it. "You're new around here, ya know. Untested." She winked and hopped out of his lap as quickly as she'd dropped into it.

Mike looked at the paper. A location for the pickup, a price, a name, and location for the drop. He had the urge to roll his eyes. Real sophisticated operation going on here. This was like passing notes in class. Anyway, he'd gotten what he came for and it was time to call it a night. He tucked the paper into his jeans pocket and dropped a few bills on the table. He was getting too old for this crap.

Chapter 5

Mike quickened his pace as he jogged the last leg of his route. The past two weeks had brought him nearer to his goal, but he wasn't there yet. His dealings with Big Jim were frustrating, but he'd earned the man's trust. In fact, twice now Jim had called Mike directly instead of following his usual protocol of handling all communication through Carl. Mike knew it had to be driving Carl crazy, and Mike hoped to work it to his advantage.

He slowed to a walk as he approached his house and called his partner. It had been a while since he'd seen him and valued his sense of humor, if not his advice.

"Hey Mike. How are things going in Nowhereland, New Hampshire?"

"Ha. Ha." Mike smiled into the phone. "It's a nice little town. I'll get you out here soon."

"Yeah, really looking forward to that."

Mike couldn't miss the sarcasm in Gary's voice.

"This quick little assignment is dragging out longer than I anticipated. We've closed bigger cases in less time." Gary reminded him. "You could always pass this off to the local DEA office."

Mike was shaking his head before Gary had even finished. "It's bigger than that. The drugs being peddled here are too sophisticated for a place so rural. The closer I get, the more convinced I am that there's more than what we see on the surface. There's a bigger fish here and I want him, too."

He checked the mailbox, more out of habit than because he thought there would be mail and realized he was starting to treat Wolf Creek as home. The people were friendly enough and the pace was so much slower than what he was used to. For the first time in a long time, cleaning up a town mattered to him.

"Aren't you the big hero?" Gary laughed but Mike knew he was only teasing. Gary, being older and slightly overweight was forever teasing Mike about his frequent undercover roles. "I hear there's a woman."

Mike groaned. Of course that would be the first thing his partner wanted to know about. "It's crazy, Gary. Her name is Rachel and I knew her back in college. We went out a couple of times and then she disappeared between semesters and I've always wondered what the hell happened to her. And here she is."

Gary whistled low. "Rachel, huh? I was talking about this Tilly woman you added pictures of in the case notes. You sayin' you got two women on the line up there?"

Mike halted on the doorstep and dropped his head. Damn! He needed to get his head in the game and leave Rachel out of it. "Not in the way you think. They're both waitressing at the bar where a lot of the deals are made. Tilly's kind of the local tramp, I guess."

"And this Rachel chick?"

"She's not a tramp."

Gary grunted. "That's good to know. But I'm more interested in how she's involved in the case." Mike could have sworn Gary was laughing at him.

Mike unlocked his front door and tossed his keys on the table inside. "As far as I can tell, she isn't."

"So why are you bringing her up? Does she recognize you? Is she a threat?"

Mike shook his head. "I don't think she's a threat and if she does recognize me she's not in any big hurry to reconnect."

Another laugh. "Do I detect bitterness in your voice, boy?"

"I haven't really talked to her yet. She keeps to herself and doesn't interact much with the players I've identified. Until she does something to put herself in my path, I think I've decided to leave her alone."

"You think so? But you might change your mind?"

"I'm keeping my eye on her." Mike muttered, imagining the knowing look on Gary's face just as Gary responded.

"Don't lose sight of the target, eh?" He cleared his throat. "So what's she like? I think you told Pam and I about her once."

Mike thought about Rachel for a minute. "She's ... genuine, in a place where that's not expected. People love her, but in a good way. Like, they look out for her or something."

"Huh."

"What?"

"You're going soft, Mike. You didn't even lead in with what she looks like. I saw the pictures of Tilly. Hello! Is Rachel built like that, too?" Gary teased again.

"Not even remotely. The women wear a uniform that consists of a white button-down blouse and black skirt. Tilly wears it like a naughty librarian but Rachel makes it look classy. Big difference between them."

"So, are you planning to use Tilly to get your intel?"

Mike scrubbed a hand over his face. "I should. I'm considering it. I noticed the other night that Rachel seems to get irritated when Tilly flirts with me. It gave me an idea that I might be able to play to my advantage."

"Irritates Rachel how?"

Mike moved his hand to the back of his neck. "A couple of nights ago I put my hand on Tilly's back and Rachel spilled a pilsner across the bar. When Tilly leaned in to whisper to me I saw Rachel nearly drop a tray of drinks on someone's table. The manager, Carl, is really protective of her, like he's staked a claim, only I know he hasn't. He calls her the Ice Queen."

Gary was quiet. Mike knew he was processing the scene to come up with a way to use the information.

"You want to use Rachel? You said she's not involved."

"She's not. But she's extremely smart and no one pays any attention to her. I bet she hears more than she knows." Mike thought about that. "Plus, if I can get close to her I could protect her from the sleezebags she deals with."

"Could be a good play. But be careful. If she's a woman scorned, she could be unpredictable."

"Another reason to keep an eye on her. I can't get a good read on her yet, but I'll add Rachel to the case notes if she turns out to be involved, otherwise I might just spend a little time finding out how she ended up way out here."

"I trust your judgment buddy. Just don't go jumping in over your head for this woman. She's already given you the drop once. She's harboring something."

Mike laughed. Sometimes Gary was more like a

big brother than a partner. "I've gotta go. There's work to be done."

Of course, flirting with both women was combustible for a whole other reason. Like a soap opera, he knew that Carl wanted Rachel, but Mike also heard men refer to her as shy and plain. Curiosity was driving him crazy because he remembered her as being open and outgoing, and so damn sexy. Since he wasn't in a position to further risk exposure by asking questions, he couldn't do a damn thing except keep an eye on her.

Like a masochist, Mike grabbed a table in Rachel's section. After days of studying her he was starting to be able to read her body language and he knew that the way he watched her made her nervous. Torturing himself, he'd found little ways to connect with her by touching her skin, holding her gaze just a hair too long, or lowering his voice to something more intimate when he spoke to her.

Tonight, Mike didn't pull any of his usual tricks on her. He knew right away that something was wrong. Rachel's face was pale and she moved stiffly as she went about her routine. She didn't smile, her face was pulled tight. Mike decided she was in pain. Had something happened to her? Had she been attacked? Or worse?

His heart pounded and he lurched forward in his chair, appraising her movements as she delivered drinks to the group at the next table. Apart from not putting off their advances as quickly as she normally did, he couldn't see anything physically wrong with her. He checked his watch. Unless she was working a double, her shift was nearly over.

Mike slipped out before anyone could engage him in conversation. Keeping a careful eye out for Jim, Carl or any of their henchmen, he kept to the shadows as he circled the building to wait for Rachel at the back door. He stood just outside of the dim lamplight that barely swept the employee lot. He wasn't sure yet if his plan was to simply watch that she made it home safely or break his self-imposed rule and involve himself in her personal circumstances.

Less than ten minutes later, Rachel emerged from the rear door. The heavy steel door slammed shut behind her and she dropped back against the cold brick with her eyes closed. Mike was debating making his presence known when the door opened again and Carl stepped out behind her. He lit a cigarette and took a deep drag while his eyes scanned the dark lot. Mike knew Carl was looking for Rachel, but whether it was out of concern or ill-placed interest, he couldn't tell.

Rachel opened her eyes but didn't visibly react to Carl's presence. Mike's hand moved to rest on the butt of his gun he kept holstered in the back of his waistband. She was a sitting duck alone with the brute in the dark.

Carl spotted her and stalked up to her, standing so close that he'd nearly pinned her against the brick. Mike narrowed his eyes, ready to intervene. Rachel appeared to have stopped breathing. Based on her pallor and the fact that she was holding her breath, Mike guessed the cigarette smoke was about to make her sick. A memory came back to him in a flash. She'd missed a lecture so he'd stopped by her dorm to check on her and found her hunched over the group toilet that bordered her tiny room. She suffered from migraines. Evidently, she had one tonight. Mike's ears strained to hear their low conversation.

"Let me take you home, Ice. You look like shit."

Rachel pressed her lips together and denied the offer with the barest shake of her head. Carl's voice shifted to an oily plea. "I can make you all better. I know just the thing."

Rachel barely opened her lips to mutter, "Thanks, but I've already got plans."

Mike thought her plans probably involved a toilet and a comfortable place to sleep, but Carl clearly took her words to heart. "With who?" he growled.

Mike couldn't have asked for a better opening. Not giving a damn for the consequences to his case or her reputation, he stepped out of the shadows. "With me."

Carl stepped away from Rachel to face Mike. He saw Rachel take a slow shallow breath out of the corner of his eye.

"Pretty sure I warned you to stay out of my territory, Black."

Mike conceded with a nod and then tipped his head toward Rachel. "In manners of work, sure. But, she's not your territory, and she's coming home with me tonight." Mike shifted his stance, casual but prepared for a fight, his hand still resting on his gun.

Carl scowled and flicked his cigarette at Rachel's feet. "This one's not up for grabs. Not by anyone. She's the Ice Queen, you know. Not even worth your trouble."

Mike's gaze switched over to Rachel and he noted that she looked on the verge of collapse. Time to wrap things up. "She looks hot enough to me and this isn't a negotiation." Mike shook his head when Carl started to speak again. "She's coming home with me tonight." He shouldered past Carl and draped an arm around Rachel's waist. He could feel her shaking under his arm. He needed to get her home. Carl's anger was palpable as he guided Rachel to his sleek black Charger and tucked her safely into the passenger seat.

As soon as he was settled and had pulled out of the lot he put a reassuring hand on her knee. She was positively shuddering now. "You're safe now, baby. But to keep up appearances, I've got to take you to my house first in case he decides to follow you. I'm sorry about that. But, you're safe with me, Rachel. I promise."

She didn't shrug off his hand and she didn't respond, but that didn't necessarily indicate her acceptance of the situation. He snuck a couple of glances at her during the short ride. Her face was a mask, her lips in a hard line.

"You okay?"

He took the tip of her chin for a nod.

They pulled into Mike's driveway a moment later. He drove straight into the garage and waited until the door came down behind them, assuring their privacy before exiting the car. He hurried around to Rachel's door, anxious to get her out of his car before she lost control and got sick. She gave him a one-sided smile when he reached in and pulled her up into his arms. She didn't weigh much and he found that he liked the feel of her warm little body cuddled against his chest as he shouldered his way into his house, setting her down in the little half bath just inside the garage entry.

"Do what you need to do. I'll be right back for you."

Mike toured the house, checking that all the windows were locked and the blinds drawn. He made a quick stop in his bedroom to give it an eye through a stranger's eyes. He hadn't planned on bringing a woman home with him so he wanted to be sure he'd picked up after himself. Deciding that Rachel probably wasn't in any shape to form judgment about her surroundings, he returned to the bathroom and tapped lightly on the door. "Rachel?"

The door creaked open revealing Rachel sitting on the floor, leaning against the wall. She was ghostly white. She had her knees up, her arms wrapped around them and her head resting lightly against her legs.

"Is there anyone waiting for you at home?" He asked quietly. His stomach clench in anticipation of her answer.

If possible, she paled even further. "No."

"I'm going to take you into my bedroom."

He chuckled at her icy look. "Tempting, but not tonight." She watched him warily but still didn't speak.

Mike hefted her into his arms again and carried her through the house. In the bedroom he paused to dim the lights and then deposited her onto the bed, trying not to jostle her. He grabbed a t-shirt from his dresser and tossed it down next to her.

He stared down at her. She was watching him with more curiosity than apprehension now. "I'm no white knight, babe. I want you too badly to stay detached while I undress you. You'll have to undress yourself." He turned to give her some privacy.

She finally spoke, her voice gravelly and low. "Renner?"

He froze and turned back to find her eyes imploring him. He couldn't very well pretend not to know her, and to her credit, she'd waited until they were alone to confirm his identity. Smart woman. "For now, it would be safer for both of us if you stick with Black, okay?"

She studied him for a moment longer, her eyes seeming to relax though the rest of her body remained stiff. "Okay."

"Can I bring you anything? You have a headache? Do you take medication for it?"

She clenched her jaw and muttered, "Too late."

Mike nodded, assuming she meant that anything she tried to take would just come back up again. "You change while I go get you an ice pack. That might help."

The minute Mike closed the door, Rachel brought her shaking hands to her chest to unbutton the white blouse that was part of her uniform. She considered sleeping in her clothes but they carried the smell of the bar, and just breathing it in make her stomach pitch. She left her bra and underwear on and slipped Mike's soft shirt over her head.

The effort it took to undress nearly sent her back to the bathroom but blessedly, her stomach was empty, so she forced a few slow breaths to settle it down. If she hadn't felt so wretched, she would've been mortified that Mike was once again seeing her in such a wimpy way. As it was, she only had enough stamina to concentrate on one thought at a time, and right now it was wishing she could fall asleep and escape the nightmarish pain.

Assuming she was meant to sleep there, Rachel crawled under the covers and got into the familiar position that often relieved some of the pain. She closed her eyes and started a careful routine of counting and breathing.

Mike quietly returned moments later. She felt the mattress dip as he sat beside her hip and placed a cool gel pack against her forehead. After a momentary rush from the shock of the cold, her pain receded just enough to allow her to relax again. Sometime later she felt Mike stretch out next to her, warming her back pleasantly. She mumbled a thanks, which he answered with a reassuring rub of her shoulder.

The next morning, Rachel opened her eyes in an unfamiliar room. Sunshine filtered in through the blinds allowing her to ease into the day. After determining she was alone in the room, she sat up and looked around. Mike's bedroom was sparse and neat. She and Anna certainly weren't as tidy. Anna! She closed her eyes, once again missing her little girl terribly. It was lucky that she was having the time of her life in Florida, otherwise last night could have been a disaster. Instead, it was…sweet.

She let the memories of the night before play out in her mind. Mike Renner, college hockey star, promising law student, and the biggest romance of her life was here in Wolf Creek. For whatever reason, he was pretending to be someone else but since she wasn't all that keen on sharing the past humble years of her life with him either, his act worked out in her favor as well. Any familiarity they had would have to remain shallow. Unless he was here to stay. She swallowed hard and looked around the room again. There was nothing personal left out. No pictures or artwork, nothing to indicate he was making himself at home here.

She smoothed the soft sheets across her legs. How long had it been since someone had taken care of her? She couldn't remember. It seemed she'd always been alone. Her parents had always been so busy with their various charities that it seemed they'd never really had time for her. It wasn't until she'd met Mike that she'd even considered the possibility of a life with someone she could be partners with. Of course, that hadn't exactly played out the way she'd hoped. And now that he was back in her life, for whatever reason he was here, she was afraid of falling hard for him all over again. How would she ever sleep again without thinking of how it felt having Mike Renner's arms around her for that one night while she slept?

Feeling only a slight migraine hangover, she swung her legs over the side of the bed and spotted a neatly folded pair of jogging pants and a zip up sweatshirt. Lying on top was a note.

*I loved spending the night with you but I thought I would
save us both the embarrassment of waking up with a
stranger.
Help yourself to the change of clothes and coffee in the
kitchen.
We can talk later. Until then —
Mike Black*

"Black," she muttered, trying out the name. If he was asking her to call him Black she had to believe there was a darn good reason because deep down she knew he was still a good guy despite bad boy appearance and matching attitude. She spent more time than she cared to admit with common variety thugs when she was working at the bar. Thugs didn't rescue women from dark parking lots, drive them home and tuck them into bed. Mike's true colors were showing. "Okay, Renner, I'll play along."

She drew a smiley face on his note and pulled on the clothes he'd left for her. She had to pull the drawstring tight to keep the pants up around her waist, but the sweatshirt was soft and comfortable and smelled like Mike. With a huge, un-Rachel-like smile, she headed to the kitchen for coffee.

After a cup of coffee, she rinsed out the pot and then headed home to start her day. Tonight, she was working the late shift so she assumed she would see Mike again, and as much as she hated the bar scene, the idea buoyed her spirits. Now that she was fairly certain he wasn't the criminal he believed him to be, she was actually looking forward to it. Knowing he wouldn't be able to pursue any serious questions of her while he was pretending to be someone else gave Rachel a sense of daring. No one there would be likely to bring up the fact that she was a single mother, so she could even relax and flirt back a little if she felt brave enough. She nearly laughed aloud as she thought of the way her co-workers would react if she were to suddenly start flirting with the customers—well, specifically with Mike.

The Ice Queen nickname had served her well over the years. It kept the creeps away and supported her reputation as a hard-working single parent, but she'd always hated it. In her past life, she'd been outgoing and fun-loving, so the image Wolf Creek had painted of her was a bad fit. Maybe now she could do something about it in a way that wouldn't hurt anyone. She was safe to flirt with Mike. Assuming he was here for some temporary reason, she could have a little fun before he was gone and she went back to being a woman on the lookout for Mr. Boring. She left Mike's house feeling excited to go to work for the first time in a long time.

Rachel's good mood had ebbed by the time she clocked in at Suds N Grub that evening. Her earlier giddiness had been replaced with nervous embarrassment. Mike was a nice guy. What if last night's act of chivalry could only be chalked up to neighborly concern, and not because he was interested in her? What if he turned her down?

Mike didn't show up until her shift was almost over which made her nearly as nervous as if he'd been there the whole time. She'd nearly given up on her plan when she spotted him. He took a seat at the bar and braced his arms against the counter. He didn't look at her, at least not when she was looking at him, and she looked at him pretty often. His seat at the bar meant that she wouldn't be the one to wait on him. Suddenly, she was thankful for that particular blessing. Now that he was there she wasn't sure she'd be able to pull off the same flirty attitude that was a natural as breathing to Tilly.

A half hour before her shift was up she'd finally worked up the nerve to speak to him, to thank him for taking care of her the night before when Tilly breezed past and threw one manicured hand over his shoulder, sliding a path across his chest.

Rachel stood transfixed barely four feet away, watching Mike flatter Tilly with his killer smile. She couldn't hear their exchange but from their body language she would guess Tilly was making her usual offer. Mike, well, Rachel knew he was really good at flirting without actually accepting what was being offered. But Tilly was beautiful and a lot of fun. Was he attracted to her?

As if he could read her thoughts, Mike flicked his dark eyes over Rachel, his expression seeming to beg her to intrude. Embarrassed to have been caught staring, Rachel flushed and resumed her trip to the bar, which brought her closer to where he was seated.

"Table ten's checking you out, Tilly."

Tilly patted Mike and gave him a wink before bouncing off to accept the attention headed her way.

"You're looking better tonight." Mike's deep voice spoke softly near her ear. She turned around and tried to take a step back but found herself blocked by the bar. Mike was in her space and the sparkle in his eyes told her he was well aware of it.

Mad at lack of bravery, she instinctively retreated into her server role. "What can I do for you, Mr. Black?"

One side of Mike's mouth lifted in a smile. "Mm. The things a man thinks of with a question like that." His gaze travelled down her body before returning to her face. "What's on the menu tonight?"

Rachel felt the blush return to her face and pressed her lips together. She was seriously out of practice and floundered to come up with a cute reply. She wondered how he'd react if she said, "Me", but Carl saved her from responding by clapping a meaty hand on her shoulder and very nearly ripping her away from Mike.

"You're not a quick learner, are you, Black? I'm sure I made it clear last night that Rachel isn't available to you."

Mike turned to Carl, effectively putting himself between Rachel and the bully. He was so close that she could feel the heat radiating off his back. Despite the gravity of the situation she yielded to the temptation and brushed her knuckles down his spine, hoping it could just as easily look like she was pushing him away rather than copping a feel. Mike tensed for a split second but never shifted his stance, never took his eyes from Carl.

"Maybe your bad memory is the problem here, Carl. I know you saw me take her home last night where she spent the night with me. In my bed. Now, I'm not the type to keep score but I think that even by your standards that makes her mine."

Beside them, Rachel saw Tilly's jaw drop giving her the sudden ridiculous urge to laugh. She didn't know whether to be mortified or relieved. Maybe she wouldn't have to flirt with Mike to shed her prudish reputation after all.

Carl tried to lean around Mike to address Rachel but Mike sidestepped him forcing him to keep his distance. She grabbed a fistful of the back of Mike's t-shirt with no plan in mind except to keep him close.

"You slept with him?" Carl roared.

Rachel wanted to dissolve on the spot. She could feel the eyes of everyone in the dining room on her as they sat, fascinated by the drama playing out in front of them.

"Rachel!" Carl roared again.

Rachel patted Mike and stepped around him. She knew the fastest way to make this go away was to address it head on, even though her strong preference would have been to avoid the conversation altogether. Mike knew her back when she was still spunky and somehow that gave her the confidence to carry out their scene in front of so many familiar faces. In a low voice, Rachel responded, "It's none of your business where I spent the night, Carl. I've been telling you this for years."

Carl was seething but Rachel held her ground between them.

"In all the years I've known you, you've never gone on a single date. Not one! One day this guy walks in and just like that, you jump into bed with him?"

Mike drew up behind her and settled his hands on her hips. It was probably only meant as a sign of possessiveness, but she drew strength from it. She flashed a quick, completely fake smile and shrugged at Carl. Inside, her heart was threatening to pound out of her chest. "What can I say? He's irresistible."

Tilly hooted and reached around Mike to offer Rachel a fist bump. "You took my advice."

"Get out of my bar," Carl growled at Rachel. He turned his anger on Mike. "This isn't over, Black!"

Mike waited until Carl had stormed into the office before spinning Rachel around and pulling her into his arms. Surely, he could feel her shaking when he nuzzled her neck, "Lock your doors tonight." She felt one of his hands brush her waist. "I'm giving you my number. I want you to text me when you're home safe."

Rachel shivered against the sensation of his breath against her ear. "My phone doesn't text."

He froze for a second. "Then dial the number and let it ring once. I'll see the missed call."

"Okay." She sighed.

Mike nipped her earlobe and released her. She slouched back against the bar and watched him stalk away.

Tilly fanned herself theatrically. "Holy crap!" Rachel faked a smile for her friend and headed to the kitchen. She'd effectively just made mincemeat of her reputation and gotten on Carl's bad side at the same time. No one could ever accuse her of doing things halfway. She dragged in a breath and lowered her shoulders to relieve the tension there.

Tiny met her at the door with his hands on his hips and a disapproving frown on his face. Rachel stopped short and blinked at him. His opinion meant a lot to her and this particular expression was one she'd never seen from him before. "What's wrong?"

He lifted his hand to wag a finger in her face. "You be careful!"

"Excuse me?" But she had a feeling she knew what he was referring to. Her blood ran cold before Tiny even spoke. Carl would cut her hours until he was done being angry with her, hours that she desperately needed. With Mike involved, Carl would now be gunning for them both. He didn't like to lose.

"You're a grown woman, and God knows you can take care of yourself. But girl, messin' around with guys like that, guys that run in Carl's crowd..." He shook his head and hauled her in for a hug. "I don't want you gettin' tangled up in that mess."

Gratitude for his caring made her squeeze him just a little harder. There were a lot of things Rachel could have said to ease his mind, like that she trusted Mike, or that she was certain he wasn't like the others. But any of those things could come back to bite her if her instincts proved wrong. So instead, she settled for the most abridged version of the truth she could manage. "Carl was bothering me in the parking lot last night. Mike must have known I wasn't feeling well so he stepped in and took me home. He stayed with me to keep an eye on me." She pulled away and patted Tiny's arm. "He's okay. I'm okay."

Tiny continued to look wary but he nodded.

"I'd better get out of here before Carl comes back for round two."

Chapter 6

It was early the next morning when Mike called his father but he knew that the man had been awake for hours, remnants of his professional life that he'd yet to outgrow. As a surgeon, Gray Renner preferred the early morning stillness and had been blessed with boundless energy.

"Mike. I haven't heard from you in a week. How's the case going? Still in New Hampshire?"

Mike grinned into the phone. "Still here. The case is dragging out a little longer than I anticipated."

"I thought this was an easy one."

"It is," Mike confirmed. "But if I'm patient I think I can reel in a bigger fish, too. I'm aiming to bring in the supplier."

"Well, you're nothing if not patient. How's Daniel?"

"I haven't seen him. I'm still undercover." Mike was quiet for a moment and even over the line Gray seemed to be able to sense that he had something more to say. "Turns out Daniel's not the only familiar face around here. Do you remember that girl I really liked in college? The one who disappeared?"

"Something with an R, right? Yes, I remember. You were so hung up on her that your mother and I thought maybe you'd bring her home to meet us."

"She's here, Dad. She lives in Wolf Creek."

"No kidding! Did you find out what happened to her?"

"That's the thing, she's still a complete mystery. Judging from the way people interact with her, she's been here a while. She's waiting tables in a bar owned by the head of the organization I'm investigating. She doesn't appear to have any family, although I remember her parents were affluent, from California. The people around here don't seem to know much about her. I can't ask too much or people will get suspicious."

"She's not wrapped up in your case, is she?"

"Not as far as I can tell. I've kept my distance so she doesn't blow my cover."

"You haven't done a background check on her?"

Mike was silent for a moment. He'd considered it. As a matter of fact, it had crossed his mind nearly every day since he first spotted her in Wolf Creek. But it would have been wrong. She had a life here and she appeared to be safe. For now, he needed to respect that. "It's tempting, but I'd rather get to know her again the usual way."

His father chuckled. "The way that involves bringing her home on a Friday night?"

It was Mike's turn to laugh. "Well, for your information, I did bring her here the other night. But, it was completely altruistic. She had a migraine and she was being bullied by her boss so I gave her an excuse to get away from him."

"You could have taken her to her own house," Gray reminded him in a knowing tone.

Mike chuckled again. "Sure. But I wasn't sure the prick wouldn't follow her there. I figured if he thought she was mine, so to speak, he might leave her alone."

"Yeah? How'd that work out?"

Mike rubbed his face. "I left before she woke up so it wouldn't be awkward."

"Always the hero."

"I should have looked for her years ago. She's different now. So guarded." Mike didn't bother hiding his bitterness, his father knew him better than anyone and probably remembered how torn up he'd been when she didn't come back to school.

"Maybe she's ashamed," Gray suggested. "She could have left school for lots of different reasons, and there's not much you could have done about it. Especially if she didn't share her troubles with you. Let go of your regrets, son. You've found her now, and once this case is over you can figure out what comes next. The chance of you happening upon this woman ten years and two thousand miles from where you met is astronomical." Gray was quiet for a moment and then cleared his throat. "Maybe your mother is meddling in heaven."

Chapter 7

"Hey beautiful. What are you doing tonight?"

Rachel was quiet. Mike's question sounded suspiciously like he was angling for a date. She hesitated. If she were smart she'd hang up on him. Of course, Anna was gone for the summer, and Mike had already played his part by demolishing her frigid reputation. Maybe Tilly was right. Maybe she should have a little fun. And what better opportunity would she get than with the man who'd been the center of her dreams for nearly a decade? "I don't have any plans. Why?"

"Any chance you're willing to help me out tonight?"

Disappointment bubbled through her. Not a date after all. "Sure. What do you need?"

"Any chance you can get me near Carl tonight?"

"Ah." Carl's schedule was a topic she knew a lot about, having done her best to avoid him for years. "He'll be at Suds tonight. It's hookup night."

On the other end, Mike laughed. "He has a regular night for hooking up?"

Rachel grinned, though he couldn't see it. "I don't think he realizes it, but Tilly and I noticed it a while ago."

"Perfect. I'll come get you. Can you be ready in twenty minutes?"

"Do I need to be there? It's my night off and I've already told you where Carl is." She knew she sounded sulky, but darn it, she'd finally gotten into the idea of dating, and now he was telling her he needed her to go back to Suds.

"Don't want to hang out with me tonight?" His voice was low and enticing which only confused her further.

"I'd love to." Great. Now she just sounded desperate.

"I have the best chance of getting up close and personal with him if you're with me."

So he wanted to incite Carl's anger? Her brain was pragmatically reminding her that this evening would turn out to be a repeat of the other night when Carl had so publicly accused her of sleeping with Mike. It was her idea of torture. But her heart was shouting at her, second chance! Second chance! Worst case scenario would be that he'd still be around when Anna came back from Florida and she'd have to tell him that she was a single parent. Anna would be so shocked to hear her was dating. "That's probably true." She sighed. "Okay. I can help."

"Thanks. I'll be right over."

The bar was crowded and noisy, but she spotted Carl right away. He had taken up residence in his usual corner seat at the bar, a cell phone plastered to his ear. Following Mike into the throng, they were able to find a table not far from the bar. Mike got the bartender's attention and ordered a couple of drinks before she told him she rarely drank alcohol. "Do you know any of the women in Carl's group over there?"

She lifted her head and peered around the room. She dismissed the surprised looks she was receiving from some of the regulars and spotted the short redhead draped against him. "Looks like tonight it's going to be Laura."

Mike looked over without moving his head. "Do you know Laura?"

"A little – not outside the bar or anything. I've waited on her a few times."

She watched Carl's expression change from annoyance to surprise to murder. Evidently, he didn't like what his caller had to say. And from Mike's expression she knew he'd seen it, too. Mike's jaw worked and Rachel could nearly feel his frustration. Something was happening, only she had no idea what.

Hearts on the Run

"I need to get close to him. Can you make small talk with his woman for a couple minutes?"

"For what? Mike, what's going on?"

"Dammit." Mike leveled a hard look at her she didn't understand and knew she was in over her head.

"I need to stay one step ahead of him." He gave her a gentle push to get her moving toward Laura. "And that's all you need to know about it."

Rachel should have been offended, except deep down, inexplicably, she trusted him. She said a quick prayer she hadn't made the wrong decision. "I don't know her that well, but I'll try."

Rachel made eye contact with Laura and her friend, Stacie, and gave them a little wave. They beckoned her over to join them. "Bingo," Rachel whispered.

"That's my girl," Mike praised her quietly, making Rachel's stomach flutter.

They wended through some dancers toward the knot of women surrounding Carl. As they got closer, Carl turned their way and scowled.

Mike moved behind Rachel, his arm draped across her shoulders lending her a strange sort of confidence and giddiness. He leaned his shoulder against the wall, putting them both in the shadows as Rachel introduced him to Laura and Stacie. After a few surprised comments about Rachel's non-existent love life that embarrassed her, they launched into a conversation about the most recent overdose at the reservation.

"It's like, what? The fourth one this year? Oh my gosh, that's just crazy!" Laura gushed.

Rachel resisted the urge to see what Carl thought of Laura's sentiments. She suspected he was indirectly responsible for the sudden upsurge in drug use in Wolf Creek. "It's scary, that's for sure." Rachel agreed.

Laura leaned forward as if that would keep Mike from hearing her. "But what about your guy? Isn't he, like, I don't know, involved too somehow?" She sized Rachel up. "We've all been drooling over your guy for a week now. I never would have guessed, well, nevermind."

Rachel could feel her cheeks burning. What was she supposed to say? She was only pretending to be on a date with Mike, but anyone who knew her could guess she didn't support didn't know what Mike was doing in Wolf Creek. Despite his false name and sudden interest in Jim's business, she suspected he wasn't really there pushing drugs. Deciding ignorance was the best course, she settled for a non-committal shrug and turned the conversation back on the other women. "So, you're here with Carl tonight, huh?"

Laura giggled and shoulder bumped her friend giving away how drunk they were. "Yeah. If he ever gets off the phone, anyway." She'd raised her voice enough to make Carl turn his head their way. He was only a few feet away but still engrossed in his call.

Rachel sensed Mike's attention was focused on Carl so she deflected as many of their questions to him as she could, hoping she was giving him the time he'd asked for. Her usually dormant jealous streak was beginning to wake and took offense to the women's interest in Mike. As soon as she realized she'd moved fully in front of him as if to block their view of him, she deliberately relaxed her stance and leaned back against him instead. Mike's hands slid around to her belly and hugged her back against his chest. Her stomach clenched at the feel of his thumbs brushing the undersides of her breasts.

She strained to overhear Carl's call as she participated in the conversation in front of her. There wasn't much she could make out as he seemed to be speaking in code but knowing the level of Mike's interest made her curious. What was he into? What was she getting herself into?

Carl's angry voice was low and urgent. Rachel's gaze flicked over her shoulder to Mike and he seemed to understand she was struggling to come up with things to keep the conversation rolling. With barely a nod to the women, he pulled her onto the dance floor.

They finished out the slow song that was playing and then returned to their table. Tonight's bartender, Tony, sent over another round of drinks. Was this her third? She'd lost track. She'd never been a drinker, and she'd probably hadn't had more than a single glass of wine since she'd left California.

She smiled and bobbed her head to the music, thinking the bar scene wasn't so bad when Mike cocked his head and asked, "Are you drunk?"

"That would be irresponsible." She giggled. "I'm never irresponsible." That much was true. Her happiness had just as much to do with finally letting loose and going out with a man as it had with the amount of alcohol she'd consumed. Letting go was a powerful thing!

"Haven't you ever been drunk before?"

She giggled again. "Never once."

"Lucky me," he mumbled with one side of his mouth turned up. He reached between them and entwined her fingers with his. She wanted to kiss the dimple on the side of his mouth.

"Yes." She nodded decisively. "There is something about you that makes me throw all my rules out the window." Mike's hold tightened and she could feel her heart beating against her breast.

"Why is that?" But before she could answer he tugged her out of her chair. "Damn. We've got to go."

He threw down a couple of bills while Rachel snatched up her purse, feeling a little dizzy. She turned to follow Mike when Carl appeared at her side and clenched a fist around her arm, jerking her back, where she bounced against his beefy chest.

"You keep your boyfriend and your nose out of my business or you're going to get the same as Tilly." Carl growled low beside her causing her stomach to pitch unpleasantly. With a slight shove, he let go of her arm and stalked back to his spot at the bar.

Rachel swiveled and turned wide eyes on Mike. She could see the muscle working in his jaw again. She didn't know what Tilly had done to anger Carl this time, but for the first time Rachel felt threatened. Seeming to read Rachel's mind, Mike took her hand again and pulled her through the rowdy group of dancers toward the door.

They passed Daniel and Savannah on their way out. Rachel tried to stop and make introductions, but Mike towed her on past without stopping. She shot Daniel and Savannah an apologetic look and saw the shock and disapproval on Savannah's face as they fled through the door.

Mike was vigilant as he walked Rachel to his car. He relocked the doors once they were inside and turned to Rachel. "What did Carl say to you?"

Rachel rubbed her hands together and looked at them. The excitement of drinking and dancing and being held by Mike deflated quickly. She was no femme fatale, she was plain old Rachel Henige and she was scared. She didn't know Mike, not really. Even in college she barely knew more about him than any other girl with a crush. He'd been the best of the best back then. But as she well knew, a lot could happen in ten years. "He said to stay out of his business or I'd get the same as Tilly. Whatever that means." She rubbed off the chill of Carl's words even though it was still eighty degrees outside.

"I haven't seen Tilly lately. Have you talked to her?"

Rachel shook her head slowly, thinking about it. "No. My hours were reduced so I haven't been scheduled to work with her lately. But she goes on benders with guys and sometimes she really makes Carl mad."

"You think that's what Carl's problem is? That you're going on a bender with me?"

"No. I mean, I've never done that, you know? I don't think he'd assume that."

"You got her number? I should call her."

Rachel looked over at him, alarm in her expression. "You think she's really in trouble?"

Mike's expression gave nothing away when he suggested, "She's been on me hot and heavy since I got here, and now I'm with you. Hopefully she's just mad."

"You're not really with me." Rachel reminded him. He gave her a look like she was missing the point, so she shrugged. "Tilly doesn't get mad about men." Looking at Mike, so serious, and so good looking she wondered if maybe he wasn't right, though. "Okay, call her then."

Mike snorted. "Pretty sure I just said I don't have her number."

He had, but hearing it again made Rachel feel better. She chewed her bottom lip and then dug out her phone and dialed Tilly's number. After four rings the call went to voicemail. Rachel left a brief message to call her back and then disconnected. She looked at Mike. "Now what?"

"Let me know when she calls you back." Mike started the car to run the air conditioning.

"So this is how the big city gangsters operate, huh?"

Mike looked at her for so long that Rachel regretted her flippant question.

"Is that what you think I am, a gangster?"

Rachel blinked at him. No, she was nearly certain he wasn't a gangster at all, but what he really was, she didn't yet know. All she knew was that Mike wasn't who he appeared. "No."

He gave her a single nod and pulled out his phone to place a call. "I need to know who Carl just talked to on his cell. Something's happening. I can feel it." Mike listened for a minute. "Thanks."

He tossed his phone into the console and turned to face Rachel. "I'm taking you home now. Lock your doors tonight and don't go anywhere tomorrow until I call you."

Rachel's stomach clenched but she didn't ask questions. Her mind was racing with so many scenarios that she couldn't find the words so she nodded to let him know she'd heard him. What had she gotten herself into? What if this, whatever this was, wasn't over when Anna came home? Would she be safe? How would she explain the changes in words that a nine-year-old would understand?

They drove to her house in silence and when Mike pulled into the driveway, he got out and walked her to the door. Rachel unlocked it and turned to face him.

"Thanks for the drinks. I hope you got what you needed tonight."

Mike nodded and then leaned in and placed a kiss on her forehead that was much too sweet for a garden variety drug dealer.

"Lock up."

Chapter 8

"The shipment's been rescheduled." Mike told Gary once he got home. "The raid's going to have to be pushed out another couple of weeks. Dammit!" Mike's team had been mobilized and was ready to arrive in town the very next weekend and now everything would need to be put on hold again.

"You think Charles is onto you?"

Mike ran a hand through his black hair. "I'm doubtful. I don't think he's calling the shots. He walks like he carries a big stick, but he's not as knowledgeable as I would have expected for someone selling in that league, you know? No way he's coordinating this racket by himself. There's a bigger player involved."

"Coming back to D.C. then? You've got testimony coming up," Gary reminded him.

Mike let out a frustrated sigh. "I don't see any way around it." He paced his little kitchen. "Leaving Rachel here unprotected from the goons she works for just doesn't sit well, especially now that Tilly appears to be missing."

Gary's voice was reassuring. "Rachel can take care of herself. You said it yourself, she's been dealing with him for years."

"Yeah, but that was when Carl still thought he might have a shot with her. Now that she's shown him she prefers me his jealousy has reached dangerous levels. He's cut her hours and he's downright hostile to her now. He watches her so closely it makes me uncomfortable."

"What are you thinking?" Gary asked.

Mike knew if he laid low for a while, or even left altogether and turned the case over to the local office, Carl would probably ease up on Rachel with time, but the agency would lose the ground he'd made in Big Jim's inner circle. If he stuck around another couple of weeks to keep the case on track, she would be safe from them all so much faster. All of Wolf Creek would be safer.

"Our original plan will still work, we can pick up Jim, Carl and the supplier. I can travel back and forth between D.C. and Wolf Creek to work with the prosecutors on the indictments. In the meantime, I just need to make sure Rachel is safe. I'll figure something out. Talk to you later."

Mike went for a jog to think through his options for keeping Rachel safe. Now that he'd destroyed her Ice Queen image he knew men would consider her fair game to swoop in and devour as soon as he left, assuming Carl didn't get to her first. He could have

Daniel keep tabs on her, but that was a lot to ask, even of an old friend. He resolutely ignored the little voice in his brain agreeing with Gary that Rachel had gotten along just fine before he'd arrived in Wolf Creek. She could certainly take care of herself. No, leaving her alone now that he'd found her was out of the question.

Compromising between leaving Rachel under Daniel's protective eye and leaving her protection up to the chief of police, who already had his hands full searching for his missing informant, Mike thought of another plausible scenario. He could send in his father. He nearly laughed aloud as the thought occurred to him. The fact was, his father was capable and there was no one he trusted more.

Making certain that no one was within earshot, he pulled out his cell phone again and placed the call. "Dad. Got any big plans for the next couple weeks?"

"Nothing that can't be rearranged. What's going on?"

"I have a job for you."

There was a pause. "You do? Or the DEA does?"

"I do. There's been a wrinkle in the timing of my case and I need to return to D.C. for a few weeks. I can't leave Rachel here unprotected."

Another pause. "You want me to be a babysitter?"

Mike chuckled. "Something like that."

"Will I be undercover, too?"

Mike held the phone away from his ear and looked at it. Gray had sounded almost excited over the prospect. "Sorry, no. You get to be you. I'm going to tell Rachel who I am. Only, in public, you don't know any Mike Black. Got it?"

"Uh, sure."

They made arrangements for Gray's arrival, giving Mike time to prepare Rachel for the intrusion of Renners into her life. He didn't lose any time calling her as soon as she got home from her day shift at Suds.

"Hey Rachel. Are you busy tonight?"

"Mike?"

"Sorry, yes. I'd like to take you out to dinner. Someplace nice."

There was a beat of silence and then, "Like on a date?"

Mike laughed. "Apparently, I've lost my touch. If you're comfortable with it, a date. I'd like to take you to Rosen's Winery."

Rachel sounded embarrassed. "I'm sorry I'm making this awkward, aren't I? I haven't been on a date in years. Rosen's is out of town. Do you want to go someplace closer?"

"No. I think we'd be more comfortable reconnecting away from prying eyes."

"Reconnecting?" Her voice was barely a whisper.

"I think it's time, Rachel. Don't you?"

She was quiet again. Longer this time. "Yes. I would love that."

"Great! I'll pick you up tonight."

"No!" Rachel gave a nervous laugh. "I mean, I'll meet you."

"Afraid that if I bring you home it will lead to sleeping together again?" He teased and then chuckled when she was silent. "That's fine. Meet me in the lot outside Pat's Grocery. In an hour?"

"Sure."

"See you soon." Mike disconnected the call, glad that no one was around to see him grinning like a randy teenager.

Fifteen minutes later Rachel stared at her reflection in the steamy bathroom mirror and willed some color into her already pasty complexion. She'd refused lots of men over the years without much regret. What was it about Mike that tore down her defenses? Last time she attributed to being young and completely bowled over by him. But now? She was a grown woman, a mother. He'd been in Wolf Creek for a few weeks and she'd seen him only a fraction of that time, and she was completely distracted by him again. She closed her eyes in silent defeat of his power over her. She still had feelings for him. It was that simple. And if he turned out to be exactly who the rest of Wolf Creek thought he was, well then she'd know she couldn't trust her own judgment.

Rachel spent the remaining forty minutes wound tighter than a rubber band ball. She called Anna in Florida but then had trouble focusing on their conversation. After the third attempt to get her mother to respond to something she'd said, Anna finally yelled into the phone to get her attention. "I'm sorry, honey. I'm just not with it tonight. Can you repeat that one more time?"

"Why aren't you with it? What's wrong?"

Sometimes Rachel wished Anna was still a toddler, completely wrapped up in her own little world. She was becoming worldly in ways that often caught Rachel off-guard. She wouldn't to lie to her daughter but her stomach still clenched as she delivered her news. "I'm going out on a date tonight."

Anna was quiet for a moment and then, "Whoa, Mom!" Rachel could almost hear Anna's grin over the phone. "Are you nervous?"

Rachel's stomach was churning. "Yeah, I guess I am. It's been a really long time since I went on a date."

"Not since Daddy, right?"

"That's right, honey. Not since your daddy."

"How will you know what to do?"

"Ah, well. I think I just have to show up and be myself." Oh heavens! How could this not turn out to be a complete disaster? What had she been thinking? Mike didn't live here, and Wolf Creek didn't have much to offer. He wasn't here to stay. That meant their little whatever-this-was, would never work out.

Anna must have sensed her mother's unease. "You'll do great, Mom! You'll have lots of fun. Where are you going?"

"We're going to have dinner at a winery in Black River."

"Eww. That sounds boring. Why don't you ask him to take you somewhere more fun, like to a movie, or swimming or something instead?"

Rachel laughed. "Well, maybe next time. I love you, baby girl."

"Bye, Mom. Have fun."

Rachel pulled her flouncy black dress out of the closet and hung it on the back of the bathroom door. The knot in her stomach settled in her chest as she remembered the time Anna had spotted the dress in her closet. She could still see her little girl disentangling herself from a jacket sleeve and appearing in front of Rachel, her face glowing. She had produced the beautiful black dress from behind her back. "This one," she'd announced triumphantly. Anna had wanted her to wear it on one of their special dinner nights to Bailey's. Rachel had worn something a little less flashy and never really had another occasion to wear it. Until tonight.

She fixed her hair, enjoying the fact that, for once, she had a reason to style it. Once she was satisfied, she applied some makeup and slipped into the dress. The dress was modest by today's standards, a long-sleeved V-neck that ended just above her knees, but it looked great on her. She marveled at herself in the mirror. She filled it out a little better than she had the last time she'd worn it but she still looked amazing.

She'd barely pulled into a spot at the back of the lot outside Pat's when Mike pulled in and parked his Charger next to her ancient Subaru wagon. Rachel wished she'd gotten out of her car and waited in front of the store for him instead. His beautiful black Charger put her car to shame. Before she was even out of her car Mike had circled his and was opening the door for her.

She felt his gaze sweep over her as she made herself comfortable in the leather seat. "God, you look hot tonight."

"Nice manners," she teased.

"Not really the image I'm going for these days. Sorry."

She gave him a quizzical look but didn't ask him to elaborate. "We could go somewhere less expensive."

"Suds N Grub?"

She made a face that made him grin. "I thought you might enjoy going somewhere outside Wolf Creek for a change. I've heard Rosen's over in Black River is nice."

Rosen's Winery was rumored to be the most expensive restaurant around. Rachel had never been there, of course, having neither the occasion nor the budget. Now she felt a little self-conscious, wondering if she really should have accepted considering they couldn't have a relationship.

As if he could read the direction of her thoughts Mike said, "Oh yeah, you're worth it."

She felt her cheeks grow warm as she met his eyes. "Thank you."

They made small talk on the twenty-minute drive into neighboring Black River, mostly Mike asking questions about various people or businesses in Wolf Creek but Rachel enjoyed their easy conversation.

He looked around the parking lot when they arrived at the tall barn-like restaurant, a habit she was surprised to realize she was already getting used to, and then hurried around to help her out of the car. It was an awfully gentlemanly action for a guy that looked so sketchy, but then she figured that in Black River he didn't have to hide the manners she knew had been bred into him as the son of a doctor and a philanthropist.

The inside of the restaurant was rustic with its high wood, stone walls, and enormous wooden beams. The tables were far enough apart to give each party a sense of privacy. Each table had a small candlelit globe to offset the dimness of the vaulted room.

The hostess ushered them to a table in the far corner of the restaurant and Rachel wondered if Mike had arranged for that particular table or if luck was somehow on his side. He waited until she was seated before seating himself and she noticed that his eyes swept the room once again before returning to hers, his hot gaze putting her on the spot. She studied her fingernails while he ordered a bottle of wine with practiced ease. The moment the sommelier left to retrieve the bottle, Mike reached across the table and pulled her fingers to his lips. The action was so unexpected that Rachel instinctively tried to pull her fingers away, but he held tight. He eyed her over their joined hands with a teasing glint in his eyes. Rachel blushed but she kept still this time. She was determined to win this battle of wills, to prove if only to herself that she was equal to his unspoken invitation of intimacy.

He smiled and laid his hand on the table between them, keeping his fingers linked with hers. "So, you work at the bar and the museum? Which do you like better?"

"The museum."

"That's better than waiting tables?"

"Infinitely."

Mike cocked his head, his eyes never leaving hers. "So why do you stay at Suds, then?"

Rachel opened her mouth and then closed it again. What could she say without exposing her pitiful past? "The museum just opened so the job's not full time yet. Savannah can't pay me a lot, but at least at Suds I can work extra shifts whenever I need to. And the tips are helpful." She shrugged. "I'm sure you noticed we don't exactly have a lot of opportunity around here."

His eyes narrowed, seeming bothered by her answer though she had no idea why. She hitched her chin and reminded herself that his opinion didn't matter. The path that led her to Wolf Creek was her own. It was her life and she didn't need to defend her decisions to him.

"You were pre-med, right? Star of the dive team. How'd you end up waiting tables on the other side of the country?"

Rachel's heart pounded its way into her throat so she took a slow breath to ease the pressure. "Life kind of sent me on some interesting twists and turns." She waved her free hand as if the years of being scared, poor, and alone with a baby to care for had been no big deal. She switched her gaze to their hands when his silent appraisal became too intense. She wished now that she'd dated, flirted, something to prepare her for tonight. Her years of being single felt pathetically obvious suddenly. As a waitress, she was a pro at short, meaningless conversation but aside from Anna, she rarely had lengthy conversations with anyone. Certainly not the soul bearing type. "I'm sorry," she whispered, feeling like a complete fool. She yanked her hand away so he wouldn't feel her tremble. "I'm not any good at this."

Mike didn't immediately respond so she stole another glance at his face. He was looking at her with a mixture of humor and understanding. He rolled one shoulder in a shrug. "We're just talking. You could ask me some questions."

"Will you answer them truthfully?"

His expression, at first surprised by her question, quickly became guarded. "When I can."

"Okay, so what do you do, exactly?"

That brought a sparkle back into his eyes. "Well, right now I'm connecting buyers to sellers of certain products."

Rachel blinked at his vague answer. "You must be pretty good at that particular skill, to have gotten under Carl's skin so quickly, huh? You certainly have Big Jim's attention, hanging out in his establishment all the time."

The smile in his eyes turned to laughter. "You have that backward, sweetheart. It's more like Mr. Charles got my attention. I represent the most powerful clientele in the world. They tend to get a little concerned about people in, ah, his line of work."

Rachel tried not to frown. She sensed that he was laughing at her.

"I like talking to you," he commented, as he took a sip of his wine.

"I can see that you do."

Instead of offering the reassurance he knew she was looking for, he continued as if she hadn't spoken. "It's not a bad career. I move around a lot so I've lived nearly all over the country. I've been all over the world."

Rachel squelched the feelings that statement elicited. Jealousy, because she'd walked away from that lifestyle long ago and she'd made peace with her decision. But the luxury of travel was something she often missed. And disappointment, because he'd unknowingly confirmed what she'd suspected all along. He didn't plan to stay in Wolf Creek.

"I don't usually stay anywhere for more than a few months at a time. Once I've done what I set out to do here, I'll be out of your hair and you can go back to turning men down in that little town of yours."

"That doesn't sound like a good life to me." She dropped her eyes to the table so that he couldn't read the feelings she was having a hard time concealing.

"What's so bad about it?"

"It sounds like a lonely way to live. Don't you ever want someplace to call home?"

"I have no reason to settle down." He answered, but something in his voice didn't ring true and Rachel looked up at him to gauge the change. There was something there in his eyes now, something deep and almost…yearning.

"Have you ever been married?" She asked him quietly.

He shook his head slowly, his eyes never leaving his face. "No. You?"

She shook her head. "Why not?"

Mike frowned at her. "It doesn't seem right to get married when I spend so much time on the road, and sometimes find myself in dangerous circumstances. That's an awful sacrifice to ask of someone you love."

Rachel shrugged. "I think love is worth a little sacrifice. If it was right, it would be worth it."

"I'm not sure most people would agree with you."

She acknowledged that with a nod. "Hence the divorce rate, I suppose."

"Especially in my line of work." He added.

"Remind me again why it was a good idea to go out with you?" She delivered the slight with a smile and one eyebrow cocked. She needed to lighten the conversation or tears would come to her eyes.

"Because I'm irresistible?"

He had her there.

Their food arrived just then and turned out to be every bit as amazing as she'd heard. In fact, the food and wine were so good that by the time Mike paid the bill and helped her to her feet, she was feeling pretty mellow.

He once again laced his fingers through hers as they walked to his car. At the passenger door she turned to face him, expecting him to lean down and kiss her. Mike looked down at her upturned face and didn't move for several long seconds. She was beginning to think she'd misread the cues and started to move away when he tightened his hold on her and pulled her into his hard chest. His lips sought hers and his tongue sank into her mouth, instantly waking a part of her that had been dormant for too many years. One hand funneled into her hair, holding her head steady, while the other slid down to rest just above her behind. She could have happily melted into his arms and continued on for hours, except she knew that sooner or later people would come out of the restaurant and see them kissing. Deciding that sooner was probably better than later, she pulled away and looked up into his eyes. "Thank you for dinner. I had a lovely evening."

"The evening's not over yet."

Rachel's heart slammed into her ribcage.

With a smile that showed he knew exactly where her mind was going, Mike clarified. "We still have the drive home."

Her breath came out on a sigh. "Right. And it's getting late. We should get going."

The return trip to Wolf Creek was quiet. Rachel was feeling awkward and unsure of herself. Her stolen glances at Mike showed that he was thinking hard about something so she didn't try to fill the silence with trite conversation.

Mike pulled into the lot at Pat's and parked next to her car. He turned toward her and put his arm over the back of her seat, sitting in silence for a few moments seeming content to just stare at her. Rachel had to concentrate to keep herself from leaning into his magnetic pull.

"Mike? Can I ask you something?" She folded her hands in her lap to keep from twisting her fingers.

"Shoot."

"What happened to you?" He tilted his head toward her. "I mean," she gave him an apologetic smile, "you didn't look like this when we were…together. You've changed."

He raised an eyebrow. "I've changed? Or my looks have changed?"

He'd asked the question seriously so she gave it serious thought. He hadn't changed, not really. He was more muscular and now sported a few tattoos. He'd traded his preppy college boy look for a rugged t-shirt and jeans. Those were physical things. But his manners still belied his first-class upbringing. Underneath the façade, he was the same man she'd known. "Your looks have changed."

He nodded and then removed his arm from the back of her seat to rest his warm hand on her knee. He stared out the windshield before flicking his eyes back to her face.

"Rachel, is there any reason I shouldn't trust you?"

Her heart lurched again. Immediately dismissing the fact that she'd left him high and dry in college without any explanation as a potential misplacement of his trust, she answered. "No."

"Then I'm going to come clean with you."

She blinked at him, her heart now racing so painfully her breaths felt more like hiccups.

"I need you to hear me out before you react. Can you do that?"

Rachel turned fully to face him, her stomach hardening into a knot. Too many thoughts and fears cluttered her mind to isolate even one. "Yes."

He rubbed his hand on her knee and looked into her eyes. "I work for the DEA honey, and I'm here undercover on an assignment. I'm impersonating a drug dealer in order to find out what Jim Charles is doing around here."

Her breath came out in a relieved whoosh. "That explains the change in your appearance?"

He smiled at her question, showing just a hint of the dimples she knew he had. "Not completely, no." He lifted his left arm off the steering wheel and tilted it up in front of them indicating the tattoo that covered his arm from shoulder to wrist. "Some of it is real." He dropped his arm back over the wheel. "This case should have been a quick one. Get in and get a feel for what's happening here. Help out Chief Mobely. If I'm lucky I can get the big dogs out of town and he can work on cleaning out the rest. Should've been a couple of weeks, tops. But now I've identified a bigger fish and it's dragging out a little longer than we expected, so while I'm involved in Wolf Creek it's really important that you keep all this to yourself." He waited for her nod before continuing. "Mobely's informant has disappeared, which escalates this case from small-town drug pushing to possible murder."

"Jay?" Rachel whispered.

Mike gave her a searching look. "Do you know him?"

Rachel put a hand over her mouth and then lowered it slowly to answer. "He–he worked at Suds for a while. I didn't get to know him well. He tended the bar sometimes. When he stopped showing up for work I just assumed he quit."

Mike shrugged. "It's possible that he did quit his job and move on. But Chief Mobely doesn't think so, and neither do I. We had a net in place and last night it all fell apart. We'll have to wait for the dust to settle before we can set up another sting. It could take a couple of weeks. In the meantime, I need to head back to D.C. to testify on another case, which means that I'm going to be out of the loop here for a little while."

Rachel felt sick. She was such a fool. She'd secretly hoped that Mike was pursuing her because he was interested in her, maybe even still after all these years. But it was crystal clear now that she was simply a convenient coincidence. She was someone he knew he could trust, perfectly positioned to give him the information he would need to close the case. Humiliation made her eyes sting and she sucked in a breath to keep the sob inside. She should have realized, but she'd been blinded by Mike's sudden appearance in town and the thrill of his apparent interest in her. She would surely cry about that later, but right now she was also relieved because she knew she could help his case in a way that practically no one else could. She cleared her throat. "Use me."

"What?"

"You need me," she repeated.

"Rachel, no." Mike made an exasperated sound. "I mean yes. I could use you. But that's not the reason I asked you here tonight." He removed his hand from her knee to lean his forearms against the steering wheel. He stared through the windshield into the black night. "I won't deny that you're in the perfect position to help this case but understand that I can do this without you. Don't offer yourself up to me as some kind of sacrifice."

She had her own reasons for wanting Wolf Creek to be a safer place, but she realized Mike couldn't possibly know that. She'd never mentioned Anna. Right or wrong, for a few weeks this summer she didn't want to be seen as a single mother. She just wanted to be herself. Rachel nodded solemnly in the dark car. "But I can listen, send you updates. Carl talks in front of me. I just never paid attention before. I didn't want to know what he and Big Jim were up to. I want to do something though. If I help you, I can make this a safer place for," she stopped herself, "the future."

He turned back to her, putting his hand back on her knee and rubbing it lightly. "I can't ask you to endanger yourself for me, or rather, for this case. And anything you give me can't be used in court."

She leaned into his touch, bringing her face closer to his. "But there's no reason that an old friend can't keep you informed of what's going on in town, right?"

Mike's hand teased under the hem of her skirt, slid up her thigh a little. "Is that what we are? Old friends?"

Rachel concentrated on not shifting into his touch. It would be so easy to get lost in the feelings that always simmered near the surface when he was around, but this was a serious topic. "Sure," she squeaked. "Friends."

He pressed his cheek to hers, his nose bumping her earlobe. "I think you could be considered a bit more than an old friend," he murmured against her neck. His breath against her ear caused goosebumps to rise on her arms. "You're more like an old flame. But still so damned combustible."

"It's been a long time," she whispered.

"But it's still there. I know you feel it, too."

Rachel had been referring to how long it had been since she'd had sex but Mike's earnest reference to the spark between them stole her breath away. "It's still there," she agreed.

Mike leaned away quickly, as if resisting temptation. "Then we'll take this one step at a time. Will you be okay to drive home?"

Rachel blinked at the abrupt change of topic but nodded. When she reached for the door handle, Mike stopped her with a heavy hand squeezing her thigh again.

"My trip to D.C. will probably last a couple of weeks. I know that my interest in you has already pushed Carl's buttons. After his threat about Tilly, I think you could be in danger."

Rachel bristled a little. "I'm not afraid of Carl. He irritates me, but I can take care of myself, Mike."

His grip on her leg turned into a gentle caress. "I know you can, sweetheart."

Rachel's heart tripped on the endearment.

"But it'll make me feel better if you're not alone while I'm gone."

They made eye contact in the dark car. "What are you saying?"

"My dad is coming up tomorrow and he's going to stay at my rental while I'm gone. He'll be here to make sure no one messes with you."

"Mike, no." She leaned away from his touch. "Don't go to the trouble." She could hear the rise of panic in her voice. "I really will be okay. I've been dealing with Carl, with all of them, for years. I'm be perfectly safe."

"Where's Tilly?"

"I don't know. What does she have to do with–?"

"Jay is missing. Now Tilly's missed a couple of shifts. Carl threatened you'd be next." Mike's jaw worked as he stared at her. "I can't take that chance, Rachel."

"I'll be extra vigilant. I can handle this. Them."

"One day I'm going to understand your insistence on being so damned independent," he warned with a hard look. "But for now, it doesn't matter. It's done. My dad will be here tomorrow and I'm bringing him over to meet you. Finally."

Rachel was quiet for a minute and Mike didn't interrupt, seeming to understand that she had something more to say.

"When do you leave?"

"Dad will get here tomorrow afternoon. I fly out tomorrow night."

Tomorrow was Monday. Anna was coming home on Thursday. Rachel swallowed, steadied her voice. It was now or never, and never seemed too high a price to pay. "So we have tonight."

Mike studied her face in the dark as though unable to believe what he was hearing. "Do you want tonight?"

If she was honest with herself, she wanted every night and she had since the first time she'd laid eyes on him. But she'd settle for just this one. She met his eyes with resolve. Too soon he'd leave and her life would go back to normal. She wanted, no, she needed, this memory. "Yes."

Without a word, Mike put the car into reverse and backed out of the parking spot. They didn't speak on the short drive to his house but he reached for her hand and brought it to his lips making her smile. Like before, he pulled into the garage and put the door down before letting her out of the car.

Mike surely had lightyears more experience than she, yet his touch gave her the impression he was just as anxious as she was.

She stayed him with a cold hand on his forearm as he unlocked the kitchen entry from the garage. "Mike?" He turned back to her. "No regrets, right?"

His lips pressed together as though to suppress a smile. "Never."

Taking the tips of her fingers in his, he led her through the house to his bedroom. Dimming the lights to a comfortable level, he closed the door and gently backed her against it. Mike's lips touched hers at the same moment that his hands grasped her hips. His fingers brushed up her sides to settle at the sides of her breasts.

Chapter 9

It had been so very long since Rachel had been touched by a man that her knees went weak when his hands teased up her sides.

She raised her hands to his chest, then slipped them over his shoulders and down his defined biceps. He felt even better than she imagined. His skin was tight and smooth, hot though the soft fabric of his shirt. She couldn't make herself stop caressing him. He deepened the kiss, pressing himself more fully against her until she could feel the effect she had on him. He lifted her so that their hips were perfectly aligned and continued his hungry assault on her lips.

Loosening his hold a little, Mike lowered her to her feet and stepped away, leading Rachel to the bed. He lifted his gaze to her eyes. "I've dreamt about you, like this, for years."

Rachel's heart melted a little more because she felt the same way. She whispered, "I haven't done this in a very long time, Mike."

He smiled and advanced on her to pull her back into his arms. "It's like riding a bike ..." She was a little intimidated by the intensity of his expression, but for the first time in such a long, long time, she knew she was safe.

Rachel had sort of expected to be ravished so she was caught off-guard when Mike lifted his right hand and feathered his knuckles along her shoulder, down her breast, settling at her waist. His movements were slow and measured, as if he was savoring the moment just as much as she was. Feeling powerfully attractive because of the way he was looking at her, she reached behind her and unzipped her dress, letting it fall in a puddle at her feet. Mike's jaw locked and his expression turned to steel, but she was not afraid. She could feel the power she held over him. His look, so dark and intense, only exposed how hard he worked to maintain his patient control.

Encouraged, she stepped forward, leaning close enough to brush her breasts against his hard chest. His arms now hung loosely at his sides as she rubbed up his arms, down again. Grabbing a fistful of his polo shirt, she tugged it over his head and tossed it onto the dress at her feet.

The sight of Mike's bare chest made her pause. He was tanned and so beautifully sculpted. The bubble inside her intensified as she realized that, at least for tonight, she was getting the chance to rediscover him.

When she reached for his waistband, he brushed her hands away and launched them both onto the bed. "You're killing me," he whispered between nibbles down her neck. "If we don't slow down, I'm not going to last."

She tilted her head back to give him better access to her neck. "I'm sorry," she whispered.

He choked on a laugh. "No, you're not. And I'm glad." A few more kisses. "But I want to do this right."

"Just being with you is right," she whispered against his lips and tugged his waistband again.

Mike groaned, but he took the hint and removed his pants and underwear before he reapplied himself to exploring her.

"We need protection," he mumbled against her shoulder.

"I'm on the Pill for my migraines." She sighed in response.

He raised himself onto his forearms and looked into Rachel's eyes, finding the truth there. Trusting him despite all that she still didn't know about him, Rachel returned his gaze openly. He'd always been the only man for her.

Mike traced a path down her body, pausing to remove her bra. He placed kisses along her breasts until he reached a tight pink nipple and sucked it into his mouth. Staying on his course, he moved down her body applying his tongue to her skin or smooth a ticklish spot until he reached her panties. With absorbed fascination, he removed those too and stared at her. Embarrassed despite how turned on she was, she tried to move her knees together but Mike stopped her with a hand on each knee and spread her legs further apart. She turned her face to the side but Mike whispered, "You're perfect."

He settled beside her, one arm cradling her head, the other gently exploring the folds of her sex, teasing and preparing her. Rachel tried to hold her focus by placing kisses along his shoulders, and down to his chest as far as she could reach him. One hand played with his soft black hair while the other traveled lower to wrap a fist around the heat of him. He groaned and pulled her hand away to place it around his neck. Without breaking their kiss, he moved over her and aligned the head of his cock with her opening and then paused.

"Look at me, baby." He whispered.

Rachel opened her eyes and found herself drowning in his. Slowly he entered her and even with the unbearable friction, she managed to hold his gaze as if he was the air she needed to breathe. They stayed that way while they made love until the pressure building inside her forced her eyes closed in surrender. Almost immediately, he joined her there, giving her his full delicious weight. After a few minutes, Mike rolled onto his side and fitted her into his chest with a huge sigh. She loved the way she felt tucked against him.

Rachel stretched a little, turned to fit her back into him and snuggled closer into Mike's warmth. "That was…"

"Yeah." He squeezed her, his arms folded around her just under her breasts. "Can you stay?"

She rolled over to stab him with a defiant stare. "You promised me the night. I get the whole night."

Mike grinned. "When you look at me like that you can have anything you want."

"Right now I just want you." She put her head on his shoulder and threw one leg over his lap. He traced the length of her hip and thigh with slow lazy strokes as they lay in the silence.

After a while, Mike tipped her chin up to look at him. He opened his hand on her cheek and rubbed a thumb against her bottom lip. "There's something about you that makes me forget everything." He was quiet for a moment. "For a woman who hasn't done this in a while, you sure are good at it."

"I'm sure your other women are much more sophisticated," she began, taking offense at what he seemed to consider a compliment, "but this is, well, this is only the third time–." She was stopped by his incredulous look. She could feel her face burning. She tugged the sheet out from under him and wrapped it around herself. The magic from a moment ago was gone. What she felt now was embarrassed and vulnerable, and she didn't like it one bit.

He sat up and threw his legs over the side of the bed and then dropped his head in his hands. He ran his hand through his silky black hair, tousling it so that it stood up in many directions. He pulled his pants back on but didn't bother to button them. She kept her eyes on her lap when he turned to face her again. She could feel his eyes on her for a minute before he spoke in a low, fervent voice. "This image you have of me, as some kind of, I don't know, man-whore, is the image I often need to present in order to do my job. But it's not me, Rachel. It's not the real me. I come on to women a lot—*for work*. But outside of a case, I expect a commitment. I don't sleep around. Besides diseases, the possibility of children is a complication I don't need."

Rachel's stomach threatened to rebel. "You don't want children?"

Mike's face relaxed into a smile. "Sure I do. I love kids and I'd love to have a couple one day. But that's a step better taken with a commitment, you know? Obviously, being gone so often doesn't give me much of a chance to have a solid relationship let alone a family."

Rachel dropped her eyes back to her lap. "True." When she met his eyes again, he was surveying her with curiosity and something very like tenderness.

"So, you're telling me I'm the only man you've ever been with?" He didn't wait for her answer but shook his head and impaled her with his dark eyes again. His phone signaled a text on the nightstand next to her but he ignored it. He sat beside her. "Rachel, what happened to you?"

Rachel opened her mouth just as his phone rang. Instead of answering she picked up his cell and offered it to him. The look on his face suggested that he knew she felt she'd been rescued by the call. "It's my partner, Gary. He wouldn't call unless it was important. I have to take this." He snatched the phone out of her hand. "Renner." His face darkened as he listened. Whatever news Gary shared wasn't good. "I'm leaving tomorrow night. That's going to have to be soon enough. My dad's coming in tomorrow to keep an eye on Rachel."

She raised an eyebrow over the way he casually mentioned her to his partner. The fact that Mike didn't have to tell him who she was made Rachel wonder what Gary knew about her.

He clicked off the phone, stuck it in his pocket, and then looked around for his shirt and pulled it on. Rachel tracked his movements from her spot on the side of the bed. He turned and squatted in front of her, taking her hands in his.

"Rachel, for what it's worth, I'm really sorry."

She tipped her head to the side. "For what?"

"I don't want you to think I'm using you. Underneath this charade, I'm a man looking for something real." He rubbed his thumbs over the backs of her hands. "I care for you, Rachel. I care for you a lot and it doesn't have anything to do with this case."

His phone vibrated again making him sigh. "I have to be in D.C. for a few weeks. If it goes well, I may be able to come back on the weekends. I know that you've made a big deal about not dating and I've pushed the envelope with you time and again. I also realize that I'm also giving you a bad reputation in town. But, when this case is over and I get to be me again, I would love to see you, to get to know each other again for real. Can we give it a try?"

The look on his face was so sincere, so hopeful, so not what she expected from a man that looked the way Mike did, that Rachel had to bite her lip to hold in a giggle. The idea of dating Mike, even long distance was so surreal, almost a dream come true that Rachel's lips quivered with the need to smile.

Her smile dissolved as the reality of the situation gripped her. Measuring her words carefully, she answered him. "When you come back, I will tell you what happened to me, why I left California. And after that," she struggled for the right way to express her thoughts, "if you still want to date me, I would love that."

Mike searched her face, seeming to understand that this wasn't the time to go into it. He went to the dresser and snatched something off the top. "I'm going to keep tabs on you while I'm gone."

Rachel rolled her eyes. "I thought we already established that your dad was going to be keeping tabs on me."

Mike sat next to her again. He was so close that his weight on the mattress tugged at the sheet she was still clutching to her chest. "Is it too soon in our relationship to say that I'll miss you and I'll want to talk to you?"

Rachel smiled. "Um, no."

"Now you can even text me." He grinned and offered her a small box.

"What's this?"

"Your new cell phone."

She swallowed back her instinctive frown and shook her head instead, forcing her tone to remain light. "I can't really afford this right now. But thank you."

Mike huffed in exasperation. "You might not be able to afford it, but I can. Take it. I need to be able to reach you, and sometimes a call just isn't convenient. Besides, this is way more fun. You can send me smiley faces and stuff."

Rachel lay the box on the sheet covering her lap.

"All you have to do is take it into Shorty's Electronics and he'll get your number and contacts switched over. I want you to do it first thing tomorrow. Are you working?"

"Yes." She stopped to think. "I'm working at the museum tomorrow."

"Good. I'm sure Harrison will be okay if you come in a little late."

Rachel did frown this time. "Daniel?"

"The other one. Savannah?"

"Decatur. They're not married yet." Then Rachel laughed. "Once they're married we'll have two Dr. Harrisons in Wolf Creek. Anyway, I mostly set my own schedule with her, so I know she won't mind. She'll probably be thrilled that I'm finally moving into this century."

Mike teased a hand down her back. Now that he was fully dressed she wondered if she should leave. "Do I still get the whole night?"

Mike seemed to relax with that one question. "A promise is a promise, and I promised you the whole night." He stood up and peeled his pants back off. Rachel didn't bother to look away. He wasn't modest and she wanted the memory of him to ward off the loneliness in the years to come.

Within seconds he had scooted in behind her and tucked her securely into his side. Placing his phone on the nightstand, he turned out the light and sighed. Rachel wiggled closer to borrow some of his heat making him groan. "If you keep wiggling like that I'll never get any sleep."

"Oh, sorry." But she wasn't. A few hours later she fell asleep with a very satisfied grin.

Waking up in a man's arms was an entirely new experience for Rachel. Those arms being Mike's made it seem like a dream. She knew the smile on her face wasn't at all sophisticated, but she couldn't help herself. For one glorious night she'd enjoyed the attention of the man of her dreams.

Rachel gently removed her thigh from between Mike's and rolled onto her back to stretch. In the next moment Mike had rolled on top of her, stretching her hands high above her head.

"Good morning, beautiful," he murmured against her neck.

"I'm glad you still think so." She sighed.

Mike pulled his head back to look at her. "You're kidding, right?" When she didn't answer, he continued. "There's nothing you could say or do that would make you less beautiful to me."

She doubted that, and her stomach churned when she realized that too soon his claim would be put to the test.

"I'm not letting you run out on me this time."

She planted her palms flat against his chest and pushed him away so that she could sit up. "I didn't run out on you. We had exams and then we both went home for the summer."

"But you didn't come back."

Rachel stiffened. She could feel humiliation stinging her cheeks. "No. I didn't come back."

Mike sat up and eyed her. "And one day you'll tell me why."

She picked at a burr on the sheet. "Soon."

"Well, I'm not going to lose track of you again. And if you ever try to run, I'll find you, Rachel. This time I have resources behind me."

Coming from anyone else she would have felt threatened, but Mike spoke the words in a way that Rachel felt deep in her heart. Was he implying that he loved her? It hardly seemed possible. But she knew that he wanted her in his life, at least for now and she would embrace that. She'd be heartbroken when he left, but she would have the memories from this second chance with him. "My life is in Wolf Creek, and I have no wish to change that. I'm not going anywhere." She yawned in an exaggerated way and moved the topic onto safer ground. "I need coffee."

"I need you," Mike growled, pulling her back down under him.

"Okay," she sighed. "And then coffee."

Chapter 10

An hour later, after promising Mike several times that she would stop at Shorty's to switch out her phone before doing anything else, he returned her to her car and left her with a kiss that she was sure she would feel for the rest of the day.

When she practically floated into the Maliut museum after going home to clean up and making a quick stop at Shorty's, she was taken aback by the disapproving frown on Savannah's beautiful face. "What's wrong?"

"I'm worried about you."

Rachel looked around the room with wide eyes, not comprehending. "What's happened?"

Savannah shook her head. "You're not acting like yourself lately. Rachel, we saw you at the bar, Daniel and I." She plunked her hands on her hips. "You were with a man!"

Rachel huffed a confused laugh. "I was, yes. His name is Mike."

"When did you decide to start dating?" Savannah looked hurt and Rachel's heart ached a little. It never occurred to her that Savannah would have cared about her that way.

"He's spent a lot of time at the restaurant lately and he asked me." She shrugged, feeling awful for lying to her friend. "There's just something about him, he's so yummy. I said yes."

Savannah's eyes nearly popped out of her head. "Did you just say he is yummy?" She looked Rachel over. "Who are you and what did you do with my friend?"

"He's okay. He's not like the other man that spend time at the bar."

Savannah looked doubtful. "I'm not so sure it's a good idea, Rach. I mean it's great that you're dating. But I think you might have started on the low end." She took another step and lowered her voice to a whisper. "I've seen him hanging around with Jim Charles and his guys. Daniel thinks they're into drugs."

Rachel couldn't quite make eye contact. "Well, I can tell you that Carl sure hates Mike."

"I guess that's one point in the guy's favor," Savannah joked. Apparently deciding to let it go, she added, "Just promise me you'll be careful, okay? You and Anna only deserve the best."

Rachel nodded. She appreciated Savannah's concern but now wasn't the time to reassure her that

Mike was a good guy. She settled instead for a half-truth. "If it makes you feel any better, he's leaving town tonight."

Savannah pursed her lips but she didn't comment.

They worked on a new exhibit for another few hours until Daniel showed up to coax Savannah into going home for an early dinner. They lived in a beautiful log cabin on the museum's grounds, but it was common knowledge among friends that Savannah could get so wrapped up in her research that she would work for days on end if Daniel didn't show up to make her to take a break.

Both women smiled at him as he let himself into the office and bent to kiss Savannah.

"Hey, what are you doing tonight?" Daniel asked Rachel.

"An old friend of my family's is coming to see me today. I suppose we'll have dinner."

There was curiosity in Savannah's eyes at the mention of Rachel's family but Daniel, she noticed, didn't seem at all as curious as Savannah at her revelation.

When seven o'clock finally rolled around, Rachel paced her living room as she waited to meet Mike's dad. Feeling like the worst kind of liar, she double checked that all of Anna's pictures had been removed from the room. It was for Anna's protection, for Rachel's own peace of mind that she'd done this, and yet pretending her daughter didn't exist felt wrong. "Everything will go right back before Anna comes home," Rachel reassured the bare walls.

No sooner had she returned to worrying about meeting Mike's dad than they pulled up to the curb in front of her house. She stood off to the side of her picture window and watched as the men exited the car and started up the walk. Mike was carrying take-out bags. She was glad for his thoughtfulness.

Gray Renner was a fit man. He looked barely older than Mike, though his hair was fading into an attractive silver. Rachel remembered a conversation long ago while she and Mike had been comparing their workout routines when he shared his father's grueling workout regimen. Time, it seemed, had not changed that.

She waited a few seconds to open the door after Mike's knock so that it wouldn't be obvious that she'd been hovering beside it, peering at them through the turned-down blinds. She drew a deep breath, let it out slowly, and then met her guests with a smile.

Even seeing them approach didn't prepare her for the wattage of the two identical smiles that greeted her. She stepped back to let them in. Gray didn't hesitate; he stepped over the threshold and pulled her into a tight embrace. Despite the obvious fact that he was a stranger to her, it felt completely natural to hug him back.

"Gray Renner." He took a step back and offered his hand.

"Rachel Henige."

"I've heard so much about you. It's nice to finally put a face to you."

Rachel smiled and then looked at Mike with one eyebrow raised. What had Mike told his father about her?

Mike held up the bags stuffed with Styrofoam containers. "Where should I set this up?"

Rachel indicated the kitchen and turned to lead them there. Mike brushed past her and familiarized himself with her kitchen by opening cabinets and drawers until he found plates and utensils. For a quick second, Rachel gave thanks that she hadn't stuffed any of Anna's things in the drawers to hide them. In less than five minutes, Mike had set the table and arranged the Chinese food selections in the center of the table.

"There's nothing scary about Chinese food around a kitchen table, right?" He whispered against her neck as he pulled out a chair for her. Across the table, Gray watched them without comment.

Mike turned out to be right. Rachel was pleasantly surprised that dinner turned out to be a non-threatening way to get to know each other. She wondered if Mike had prepped his father because he never asked a single question about her family, her education, or even what her accomplishments were, which would have been the usual way to get to know one another. Instead, every question, every conversation revolved around the present. Mike urged her to share details about each of her jobs and about her schedule in such a way that she didn't feel pressured or put on the spot. Gray had such an easygoing manner that it seemed a smile was always lurking around his lips. He was easy to talk to, probably because he was such a good listener. She suspected Mike was like that when he wasn't on a case but so far she'd only ever seen him playing the part of a hardened criminal. Well, until last night. He'd been plenty playful then. She blushed and focused on her food.

When the food was gone, Rachel stood to load the dishes into the dishwasher, but Mike beat her to it. She caught his eye to give him a warning look, but with a wink he whooshed her plate away and rinsed it before loading it, correctly, into the machine. Gray didn't seem at all surprised at his son's behavior. In fact, once Mike had removed the dishes from the table, Gray took care of the food containers.

Transitioning the conversation to Gray's responsibilities while he was in Wolf Creek, Mike turned around and leaned against the counter with his arms folded over his chest, a dish towel slung over his shoulder.

"I'm flying home tonight and I'll probably be in D.C. for two weeks. During that time, Dad is going to stay at my rental." Mike's expression was serious. Rachel had heard all this already and she suspected his father had, too, but since he was in full federal agent mode she didn't interrupt. In fact, she was a little turned on by his take-charge attitude, maybe because she knew he was doing this because he cared about her.

"Dad's going to check in on you. A lot." Mike looked from Rachel to Gray. Gray nodded. "If you have to go anywhere except between here and the bar, he's going to go with you."

"Even to the museum?"

"Yes. Even to the grocery store. He's going to be your new shadow."

"Mike, this is unnecessary. People are going to get suspicious. I don't have visitors. Most people know I have no –" Rachel faltered and tried again, "no family."

"You never dated before either. Well, now you do both. You'll have to introduce him as–"

"I've already mentioned to Daniel and Savannah that I have an old friend of the family here to visit me. Savannah looked so surprised. If I introduce him as family, that's just going to open my life up for even more scrutiny." She turned to Gray. "It is unbelievably chivalrous of you to come all this way to protect me but it's really not necessary."

Mike's expression hardened. "Rachel, this is not negotiable. I've put you in danger. Hell, you were probably already in danger and didn't even know it. My dad is here and he's going to keep an eye on you."

Rachel stepped up to Mike and jabbed a finger in his chest. "I have a life to live in this town! When the case is over you'll leave and I will still be here."

Mike wrapped a fist around Rachel's fingers to stop her from poking him and stared down at her irate face. His expression softened.

"Okay." He transferred his gaze back to his father. "Here's how we're going to play it. You're going to give my dad your schedule and he's going to follow you. He won't go with you and he'll only step in if he thinks you're in trouble. You don't have to talk to him, and no one will know he's here for you."

Rachel let out a frustrated sigh. It was a fair compromise, but she was being terribly rude to Gray. She turned to him. "I'm sorry, Mr. Renner. I don't mean to be rude or seem ungrateful for what you've come here to do. It's just, it's a lot to explain. I live a very private life. I've worked really hard to create a certain image so that people would leave me alone. I'm worried that if you show up now and I introduce you as family, people are going to start asking questions." Rachel felt her face burning. She'd gone too far, practically admitting that she was concealing something from them.

Perhaps as a physician Gray was used to dealing with uncomfortable situations, maybe even secrets, and that was why he didn't comment on the end of her diatribe. Instead, he looked from her to Mike. "That's fair," he conceded. "You can give me your schedule and I will just drop by now and again to check on you."

Rachel opened her mouth but Mike stepped away from the counter with a firm, "That's all you're going to get."

While Mike got Gray set up with Rachel's phone number, Rachel copied down her work schedules and some of the other errands she usually ran. Gray accepted it with a look of amusement in his brown eyes. "Your safety is Mike's priority."

"Unnecessary. But thank you. He's a good man."

Gray smiled and Rachel couldn't help but adore him. So far he'd proved to be patient and kind-hearted, and seemed to bear his son's orders with a great deal of humor. She wondered if he'd still show that same humor when her past was inevitably thrown in their faces.

Mike checked his phone for the time and announced that it was time to leave. He had a flight to catch.

Gray excused himself with another hug and a reminder that he was always just a phone call away, and then headed to the car to give them a few minutes' privacy.

The instant the door closed Mike pulled Rachel into his arms. "I'm going to try to call you every night. And you can text me. If you need anything, anything, call me or call my dad, okay?"

"Like a booty call?"

Mike held Rachel away from his chest to give her an incredulous look which melted into a grin. "No. For that you'll have to wait until I get back."

Feeling brazen, she snuggled back into his arms. "If you say so."

"Screw that, I'll come back this weekend."

Rachel giggled.

With one last unforgettable kiss, Mike bounded down the sidewalk to his car. Rachel closed the door and brushed away the tears. "This is going to be bad. Really, really bad," she muttered to herself, and locked the door.

Chapter 11

For the first time in her life, Rachel was glad she had two jobs to fill her time. With both Anna and now Mike gone, her life had gone from sedate to nonexistent. Mike was true to his word and called her Tuesday night as soon as he got out of court, and on Wednesday he texted funny comments between court sessions. He shared pictures of his townhouse near D.C., and his cat, whom an elderly neighbor often cared for when he travelled.

Feeling bad that Gray had come all this way to be alone in a small town, Rachel called him on Wednesday evening and invited him to dinner. He answered on the third ring and Rachel had the fleeting humorous thought that he was sitting in his car outside her house. "Mr. Renner?"

"Gray, please."

Rachel cleared her throat and resisted the urge to look out the front window. "Are you busy tonight?"

Gray laughed. "Not unless you are." There was a brief silence and then, "I'm kidding, dear."

She released a breath. "Oh. I wanted to take you out to dinner tonight. Bailey's on Main Street is the closest thing we have to fine dining. She has an excellent Yankee Pot Roast."

"You don't have to ask me twice. What time do you want me to pick you up?"

Rachel laughed. "Soon. I'm starving."

Sounding a lot like Mike, he answered, "I'm on my way."

As Gray smiled at her from across the table, Rachel realized she was glad for the chance to get to know him. For just a moment she felt a stab of loss, missing her own parents and her sister. In Gray's eyes she found openness, a sort of forgiving countenance that made her jealous of Mike. If she had gone back to school, would things have worked out between her and Mike? Gray could have been her father-in-law now. What would her life have been like with men like the Renners to depend on?

A few older couples Rachel knew in town stopped by for introductions. She felt fairly confident that she'd managed to pull off the lie that Gray was an old friend of her family's. Gray handled the situation with ease. At least when everything fell apart for Rachel, the people in Wolf Creek might remember that the only relative they'd ever met was a handsome, classy guy.

Practicing what Mike had suggested during their date just a few days prior, Rachel kept the conversation focused on Gray.

"Do you have any hobbies now that you're retired?"

Gray chuckled, probably over her awkward conversation skills. "I go running nearly every day. Occasionally I give lectures to surgical residents. I guess you could say I'm still easing into this whole retirement gig."

Rachel smiled. "Do you golf?"

"A little," he conceded with a nod. "I'm not very good."

"Neither am I. I hear there's a decent course in Black River though. In case you feel the urge."

"I was thinking of hiking some of the trails before I head home."

"I've done a few of the trails over by the reservation. It's beautiful out there and well-kept now that we have a resident park ranger living here. Bailey's husband does Search and Rescue for the National Park Service."

"That's got to be a rough job."

"I imagine so." She looked toward the kitchen where she could see Bailey smiling up at her seriously good-looking husband. "He seems happy though."

"Maybe we could hike a trail together before I leave."

Rachel nodded, trying not to think about what his leaving would feel like. She compared the pain of loneliness with the pain of losing people she loved. The difference, she decided, was that letting people in her life brought happiness along with the pain and it occurred to her that perhaps by protecting herself all these years she'd really only been hiding from the pain. "I would like that."

Gray steepled his fingers over his plate and studied her. "You're really guarded for someone so young. But I sense that's not your true nature."

Rachel stared at him from across the table. "You're very perceptive."

He held up one hand. "Father of a federal agent."

Rachel laughed. "I used to be very outgoing. Being alone tends to suck the gregariousness out of you."

"Have you been alone by choice? Or by circumstance?"

Rachel had really never allowed herself to consider it because to know the truth would mean facing the chance that her decision has been the wrong one. "At first by circumstance. At some point that became by choice."

"Don't you want to marry, have a family someday?"

"Not all women do."

Gray sat back, apparently enjoying the verbal maneuvering. "True. In my profession I know lots of career-minded women. But you seem like a natural caretaker."

She smiled. "That's probably the only thing I enjoy about waitressing. I love chatting with the families that come in for lunch and dinner. I love it when old Mr. Fritz comes in and orders a steak medium-rare when I know that he's supposed to watch his cholesterol. I love when Mrs. White orders mozzarella sticks when her dentures don't fit right. It's silly, but I know my customers, and I love knowing that I can do some little thing to make life better for them."

Gray's eyebrows drew down. "What do you do for them?"

"I tell Mr. Fritz that Tiny's trying out new recipes and that we really need his opinion and then I serve him something that fits into his diet."

Gray barked out a laugh. "That's downright devious. On behalf of heart surgeons everywhere, we thank you."

Rachel grinned.

"What do you feed Mrs. White?"

"Oh, she can have the mozzarella sticks. But I cut them up and have Tiny make them extra crispy so that they don't get stuck in her teeth."

"That's just brilliant. Your customers are lucky to have you."

"I'm lucky to have them, too. Some of them really brighten my day."

"And some of them not so much?" Gray asked in a knowing tone.

"Mostly anyone that walks in between happy hour and closing time."

Gray chuckled. "Not into the bar scene, huh? Mike isn't either."

"Really?" Rachel frowned remembering all the evenings she'd seen him there. Though, come to think of it, he'd only come in when Carl or Big Jim were on the premises.

"He prefers more solitary endeavors."

"Unless he's playing hockey."

Gray nodded. "Unless he's playing hockey. Then the gloves come off, so to speak."

Rachel smiled to herself, remembering all the games she'd attended, not because she enjoyed or even understood the sport, but because she had the biggest crush on the guy that played center.

"He was something else, wasn't he?" Gray asked softly.

Rachel met his gaze. "He still is."

Gray seemed to feel the weight behind her words and reached forward to squeeze her hand before settling back in his chair and reaching for the bill.

Rachel reached forward to snatch it out of his hands, but he held it out of her reach with a look so familiar that she nearly smiled. "I'm old school, so humor me and let this old man pay for dinner."

"All right. But next time it's on me."

"Sure, sure," he agreed, but they both knew he didn't mean it.

Rachel checked in with Gray the next morning to let him know she was making a trip into the city and politely but firmly declined his offer to go with her. She assured him she'd be perfectly safe leaving town. She promised to text him the moment she got back into town. She also stopped in to visit Savannah before she headed to Concord to pick up Anna from the airport.

Savannah beamed at her friend. "You're practically glowing. You must be so relieved to have Anna home. I know I've missed the little squirt a lot. I can't imagine how you are feeling."

"Excited. But I've got to see her getting off the plane first! Then I can relax. Right now I'm a basket of nerves that she missed her flight somehow, or that something has happened to her. It's crazy feeling so emotional about something people do every day. I feel like I could cry."

Savannah exchanged a look with Daniel and then asked, "So have you heard from that Mike guy lately?"

Rachel's stomach lurched and she took a moment to feel it settle before responding. "Yes. I talk to him every day. Why?"

"I was just wondering if he's coming back to Wolf Creek."

"She was just being nosy, that's all," Daniel added.

"I was worrying," Savannah clarified.

Rachel managed a smile, though her stomach was still rolling. "It's okay, Savannah. He's okay. I'll bring him around so you can get to know him. Soon, I promise."

Chapter 12

Rachel pushed the speed limit all the way to the Concord airport. It was more than an hour's drive in normal traffic, but she managed it in just under forty-five minutes. She was an hour early for Anna's flight just to be sure that she'd be there if the plane was early.

Anna was coming home a week earlier than her friend Emma, so Emma's grandparents had arranged for Anna to have a non-stop flight home. Rachel was anxious but she knew that Anna was excited to be traveling alone. She was such an adventurer.

She located the gate and snagged a seat to settle in and wait. She pulled out her phone and checked for any new texts from Mike. Nothing.

She knew he'd be tied up in court for most of the day, but it would have been nice to have some little note from him to distract her while she waited. She pulled up a game on her phone, inwardly cringing that she was turning into one of the phone-obsessed people she'd always turned her nose up at.

The game was not enough to keep her worries at bay. Anna was coming home today. Mike was hoping to come back tomorrow for the weekend. Plus, Gray was here to keep an eye on her. How could she possibly explain why she hadn't mentioned Anna? How would she explain them to Anna? Did it even matter? Lots of single parents dated. She'd already told Anna she'd gone out with Mike. Surely, she wouldn't find it strange or upsetting if Rachel spent more time with him. And Anna had never met any other family. She could easily carry on with the story that Gray was a family friend. Oh God, when had this become so complicated? She was lying to everyone to protect her stupid pride and any day now it would all come tumbling around her feet.

Those worries led to the realization that when Mike's case was over and he stopped coming around, she'd probably be stuck making up a story for Anna about where he'd gone, too. All of that didn't even begin to cover what her co-workers at Suds thought about her dating one of Bill's minions. No matter how she looked at it, she knew that the general public of Wolf Creek would believe that she'd been dumped by a good-for-nothing drug dealer.

Anna's flight arrived just a few minutes late and Rachel found herself bouncing on her toes as she peered through the passengers departing the jetway into the terminal. There, with a huge smile on her face, she spotted her beautiful, black-haired daughter.

As soon as they were close enough to reach, Anna launched herself into Rachel's arms nearly knocking her off her feet.

"It's so good to have you back, baby girl. I missed you so much!" Rachel mumbled into Anna's hair. Anna hugged her hard before leading the way to the baggage carousels, showing her mother how adept she'd become at traveling.

Anna kept up a steady, mostly one-sided conversation as they collected her bags and made their way to the car and then home, with a stop at Bailey's for lunch before returning to the house. Rachel knew that soon their house would go from tidy to tornado survivor in as much time as it would take for Anna to walk from the entry to her bedroom. She smiled. It was good to have her girl home.

During dessert Rachel received a text from Mike saying that he had a surprise for her and asking if she missed him yet. Miss him? She'd thought of nothing else since Monday. Surely that didn't make her a bad mom? How angry will Mike be that she'd never mentioned being a single parent? And what would Anna think of Mike? Without examining her motives too closely, Rachel acknowledged that she would give nearly anything for Anna and Mike to hit it off.

On the way home she reached into the backseat for Anna's hand and gave it a squeeze. "I'm glad you're home, sweetie. I love you."

Anna pulled her mother's arm into a fierce hug. "I love you, too, Mom. And I really have to go potty!"

Rachel chuckled. "All right. We're almost home."

Rachel pulled into the driveway, put the car in park and then sent Gray a quick text letting him know she was home safely. Leaving the luggage in the car for now, Rachel and Anna hurried to the door. Rachel had the key in the front door lock before she realized something was wrong. The first thing she noticed was that the blinds in the windows facing the road were disturbed. She never left them crooked. Even when Anna adjusted them, Rachel came along behind her and straightened them. It was one of her pet peeves.

She wiggled the key in the lock confirming what she knew in her gut to be true. The lock had been broken. Her heart began to race and she felt the suffocating rush of panic racing through her limbs. She turned Anna around and ushered her away from the windows.

"No. I have to go, Mom," Anna whined.

"I have a bad feeling and I don't think we should go in right now. Can you stay away while I take a look inside?" Anna nodded and Rachel could see she was struggling to be brave even while she didn't understand what was going on.

She pushed the door open slowly and peeked inside. The living room had been completely destroyed. Her heavy old couch had been overturned. Framed photographs and other small objects had been thrown and were spread across the room in piles of broken glass and splintered wood. Tears sprang to her eyes and she pulled the door closed with a quick snap.

"Should we call the police?" Anna asked.

"I will," she reassured her. "I just need to see what's going on first."

"Make sure they didn't take my daddy's ring." Anna told her anxiously. "It's really valuable."

Rachel closed her eyes and then opened them again. That ring, and a scrapbook, were all that Anna had of the father she'd never met. Rachel dearly hoped they hadn't fallen into the wrong hands.

"Run next door and ask Mr. Peters if you can use his bathroom. And then stay there until I come get you. You can tell him all about Florida."

"You just want me out of the way. But I'll stay for a little bit." She added when Rachel gave her a look.

Rachel waited until she saw Mr. Peters let Anna in and then stepped over the threshold to survey the damage. She checked the kitchen and found that the drawers had been emptied onto the floor. Cupboard doors were open, the contents dumped and scattered across the counters. She didn't have much of value and she knew that what she did have was kept in her bedroom. She headed there next.

Rachel's bedroom had been thoroughly tossed. Every drawer, every closet shelf had been emptied. Even her mattresses had been flipped and shredded. She squeezed her eyes closed and fought the panic attack threatening to overwhelm her. She went into the bathroom and peeked into her jewelry drawer. The few pieces she had were still there. She hadn't been robbed.

She checked Anna's room next. It was usually messy, but one glance at the disorder and she could tell that room had been searched, too.

She dug around in the closet and retrieved the photo box that contained a small album, a man's t-shirt and a sports ring. It had been opened, but the contents were intact. Whoever searched her house hadn't looked too closely at Anna's memorabilia. Rachel let out a sigh and swallowed down the acid burning its way up her throat.

"Maybe it's just a mean prank," she whispered to herself.

Despite her attempt to reassure herself, Rachel was most bothered by the fact that nothing appeared to have been taken. If she hadn't been robbed then what were they looking for? Could Big Jim's thugs have been looking for information on Mike because he'd left town so suddenly? Did they think she's stolen something from them? Perhaps someone just wanted to scare her. She hated not having the answers. She knew she had to call Gray, and that he would immediately call Mike. And once Mike came back from D.C., things were going to change.

Rachel went next door to talk to Anna. Old Mr. Peters let her in immediately.

"I didn't see anything going on there today, Rachel," he explained in an apologetic voice. "I had an appointment this morning and I barely got back before you did. I surely would have called Chief Mobely."

"I know," Rachel assured him. "It's okay. Probably just a mean prank." She patted his arm and then turned and squatted down in front of Anna.

"I'm going to call a friend to come over and have a look at this. I'd like him to come look at this with me. Then we'll call Chief Mobely."

Anna nodded with huge eyes and moved into her embrace. "Momma, I'm scared."

"I am, too, baby." Rachel knew Anna was feeling insecurity. Because of Rachel's careful, low-key lifestyle, it was something Anna had never experienced before. An unknown person had been in their house and gone through their things. Her home had been violated.

Rachel left Anna sitting on Mr. Peters' couch and went outside to make her call. "Gray? Can you come over? I've just gotten home and found that my house has been broken into."

"Don't touch anything. I'll be there in ten minutes."

He arrived in five.

Rachel waited on her front stoop as Mike's Charger pulled up to the curb. Her heart dropped into her stomach when she realized he wasn't alone. Mike was with him. Why wasn't he in D.C.? And, oh crap! Anna was right next door. She hadn't planned for Anna to meet Mike and his father this way.

Mike bolted out of the car and pulled Rachel into a fierce hug, his hand on the back of her head pulling her face down into the curve of his neck. "I'm so glad you weren't home when it happened," he whispered into her hair. Releasing her, he was all business in the space of a heartbeat. "Have you called the police?"

"No. You said to call your dad first if anything happened." She looked him over. He was still dressed in a suit and tie. He must have just gotten in. "What are you doing here?"

Mike turned back and looked at her with incredulous eyes. "You were in trouble."

"No, here in Wolf Creek. You're supposed to be in D.C."

A brief smile creased his face. "That was my surprise. I was able to get away early so I came back to see you."

Rachel blinked and then followed him into the house. She watched as he looked around the living room with narrowed eyes. She didn't provide any theories, knowing him well enough by now to understand that he would want to see for himself what they were dealing with. There would be time later for questions. Mike loved questions.

"Was anything stolen?" His expression was serious, almost deadly, and Rachel realized she was seeing the side of him that her friends and neighbors must have seen all along.

"Not that I can tell." She wrapped her arms around her middle for security.

"Did you keep any notes, anything that might have put my case in jeopardy?"

"No, nothing."

Mike pressed his lips together and nodded. His face seemed to soften when he turned to look at her. "I'll call the chief in a few minutes. I have a couple of questions first."

Rachel choked out a laugh. "Of course you do."

Even Gray chuckled.

"Did Tilly ever mention being broken into?"

Rachel frowned. "No. But I haven't seen or talked to her in a while."

Mike started toward the kitchen when a soft voice stopped him.

"Mom?" Anna peeked around the corner from the living room. Her expression told Rachel she'd heard every word. Knowing they would be safe now that Mike was here, Rachel held out her arm and Anna rushed forward to bury herself in her mother's side.

Rachel stole a look at Mike's face and sucked in a breath at the fire she saw there.

"Mom?" Mike echoed. "You have a…" His mouth snapped shut. He shook his head and started again. "Is this what we were going to talk about? You didn't bother to mention that you have a daughter, Rachel? Why?"

Rachel saw Gray look from Anna to Mike and when he locked eyes with her, she knew he'd put the pieces together. Her eyes begged him not to say anything. Not in front of Anna. Not like this. Gray gave her a nearly imperceptible nod and she closed her eyes in relief. She moved her arm up to Anna's shoulder protectively. "Mike, Gray, this is my daughter, Anna."

Mike had yet to recover his speech so Gray stepped forward and gave Anna a hug. "It's really nice to meet you, Anna. I'm Dr. Renner."

They all looked at Mike, expecting some sort of greeting, but his eyes were only for Rachel and they were angry. Gray chuckled and towed Anna along by placing a gentle arm around her shoulders. "Why don't we go outside while your mom and Mike finish their conversation? Will you show me around your backyard? You must have been away recently. Will you tell me about it?"

Rachel watched Gray lead Anna through the back door and swallowed against the painful lump in her throat. She could feel Mike's gaze burning into her skin. She turned to look out the window over his shoulder because she couldn't bring herself to look him in the eye.

"You've been hiding a kid?" His voice was strained. "I don't understand. Lots of single women our age have kids. Did you think I wouldn't spend time with you if I knew you were a mother?"

Rachel remained silent. Was this the right time, the right way to tell him? With Anna ten feet away?

"Answer me. Do you think I'm so shallow that I couldn't fall for a woman with a kid?"

"This," she waved a hand between them, "has never been about dating. We were together because of your case. Anna's not material to your case and I wanted, I needed, to protect her from that." Rachel pressed a fist to her chest. "She's all I have, Mike. She's my whole life." Her heart pounded as she struggled to maintain her composure.

"Did you ship her away when I started paying attention to you? Where's she been all this time?"

"No. She had the opportunity to spend most of the summer with her best friend in Florida."

Mike's eyes narrowed and burned into her. "Is that why you finally caved and agreed to go out with me? Because she was gone, and you felt like exploring that freedom?"

"No! It wasn't like that."

"What was it then? Why couldn't you have told me you have a kid?"

"Anna —" she began and stalled.

"Where's her father?" Mike ran a hand through his hair.

"She doesn't have a father."

He gave her a narrow-eyed frown. "Immaculate conception, huh?"

She ignored the harsh sarcasm in his voice. "I mean he's never been a part of her life."

Mike stalked toward the front window and she saw his shoulders hitch. He turned around slowly, suspicion in his eyes. "How old is she, exactly?"

"She's nine."

Rachel could see him doing the math and knew when he'd arrived at the correct conclusion. She held out her arms in a gesture of apology. "Our study weekend yielded more than a good grade on the final."

Mike stared at her in shock for just a moment before turning to the overturned couch and giving it a violent kick that set off a chain reaction of shattering glass and ringing metal as broken objects scattered across the floor around them.

Gray cleared his throat to gain their attention and was rewarded with the attention of two pairs of turbulent eyes. "I see you're not done yet. Is it okay if

I take Anna for a ride in your very cool car, Mike?" He turned to Rachel. "And then I think we'll go for ice cream. Give you two time to wrap things up here."

Rachel nodded. "Yes. Thank you, Gray." She pulled Anna into a quick hug. She sneaked a quick look at Mike over Anna's head and saw him studying the girl.

"Beautiful girl," Gray commented to Mike. "And so bright! You must be really proud of her."

"I am."

"Mike, you'll have to hear about Anna's adventures this summer."

Mike managed a stiff nod.

Anna beamed up at her mom. "Dr. Renner is taking me to that little shop where they dip the cones in chocolate!" Anna's enthusiasm in the face of such a frightening experience brought hot tears to Rachel's eyes. When you're nine, ice cream still fixed everything.

Gray took Anna's hand, led her around the shambles of their living room and commented, "You know what, Anna? Why don't you just call me Grandpa? Dr. Renner just sounds stuffy, doesn't it?"

Anna's smile couldn't get any wider. "Cool! I've never had a grandpa. But all my friends do. Except for my friend, Peyton. Her grandpa died when she was just a baby."

Gray laughed. "Well, you've got one now."

Chapter 13

Mike spun back to Rachel as soon as the door closed behind them. "What the hell, Rachel?"

She turned to face him but didn't offer an explanation. She'd kept the circumstances of Anna's conception such a complete secret that she'd never spoken of it, not even to Buzzy, or Tilly and Tiny, who were the closest thing to family she had in Wolf Creek.

Frustration was evident in the way he repeatedly ran his hand through his hair, and a little of something else in his eyes. Pain? Regret?

"You're sure she's mine?"

Rachel tamped down her instantaneous anger. They hadn't known each other long at all when she got pregnant. It was fair to ask. Still, she couldn't keep the indignation from her voice when she reminded him. "You're the only man I've ever been with."

Mike took several seconds to assimilate that. Then his eyes narrowed again as he took a few steps closer. Rachel resisted the urge to back away, knowing it would be childish to hide. He was radiating anger and she felt she deserved the brunt of it, but she wasn't afraid of him. "You're telling me that you've known I am her father for *nine* years and you never bothered to tell me? What were you thinking?"

She hugged her arms around her middle and steeled herself. Her noble actions in light of his reaction only seemed selfish now. "I was thinking that I'd already ruined my life. I couldn't bear to ruin yours, too."

Mike's anger simmered into a look of such profound disbelief that Rachel rushed to make him understand. "The semester was over and you'd gone home for the summer before I even realized I was pregnant. That next semester was going to be our hardest. I had residency coming up, and it was your last year in law school. You were so popular and at the top of your game in hockey." She closed her eyes as the memories of their weekend together washed over her. Tears spilled down her cheeks when she opened her eyes again. "You had your whole exciting life ahead of you. No way was I going to get in the way of that."

Mike sat on the up-ended couch, the enormity of her sacrifice written on his face. He rubbed a hand over his jaw. "You didn't try to finish your residency?"

Rachel couldn't speak. Long buried memories had formed a painful knot in her throat.

Mike shook his head. He looked ill. "How did you end up here, Rachel? Tell me the rest of it. I need to know."

She tried to swallow. "I told my parents. I actually expected they'd be supportive, help me find childcare, set up a place to live. They do that very thing so often for charities they support, you know? But they were angry. So humiliated. They insisted on knowing who the father was. They were so upset that I honestly thought they might try to sue you for assault or something. I couldn't let them do that to you. I refused to give them your name, so they called me a tramp and invited me to leave." She tried to shrug but her posture was so rigid that the motion didn't come out right. "I couldn't work enough hours to support myself and complete my residency, so I had to make a choice. I chose Anna."

Mike was pale now. He stared at the floor. She knew he was hurting and hated herself for it. There was nothing to be gained by sharing her story, nothing could come of it but more pain, but she carried on.

"I cashed out my college savings, packed a bag, and hopped a bus." She gave a dry laugh. "It's so cliché. But a bus ticket couldn't be traced and I didn't particularly want to be found." She looked around her wrecked home remembering when she stepped off that bus. "The bus driver took pity on me and got me a room at Buzzy's Bed and Breakfast for the night. Buzzy was so sweet and understanding. She let me stay with her until I could find a job. The next day I met a wonderful woman, I think you've met June? She was working at Suds even then and she waited on me. She was so encouraging. She seemed to know I was on the run so to speak, but she never once asked me what I was running from." Rachel smiled at a baby picture of Anna that lay on the floor near Mike's feet. "Of course, the reason became obvious soon enough. It was nice here. She got me a job. The cost of living was low enough that I was able to make it work. I figured Big Jim only hired me for my looks, and maybe because Tiny threatened to quit if he didn't give me a job. I'd never waited tables a day in my life! But Tiny and June took me under their wings, showed me the ropes, and protected me from–." She drew in a quick breath when Mike stiffened. She didn't want to remember how scared she'd been when she first started working for Carl. The sneers and wandering hands! She shuddered.

"By the time Anna was born I had established a reputation for being cold, and I've clung to it, always. I've never dated. Not once since I left California have I accepted an offer from a man. Until you came. I must be the biggest fool on earth." Rachel gave a dry laugh that ended in a sob. She took a breath.

"You should have told me." Mike's voice was low, serious. "I could have helped, made things easier for you."

Rachel shook her head before he'd even finished. "No. You would have resented me. We were so young. Too immature to make it work between us. And we barely knew each other."

Mike opened his mouth to speak but Rachel interrupted him again. "You were so smart, Mike. And ambitious! You were gorgeous and fun. And on top of all that, you were a genuinely good guy. I couldn't take all that away from you because of one stupid mistake."

"But it was our mistake, Rachel. You didn't create Anna alone." He held up a hand to stop her when she started to speak. "You made all the decisions and faced all of the fall-out alone. But you didn't have to. I would have been there for you. Your parents might not have supported our decisions but mine would have. My mother would have moved heaven and earth to help us. She would have laughed and said our timing was poor, and then she would have welcomed Anna into our family with balloons and flowers and open arms." He stood and began to pace. Rachel could see that he was getting angry again.

He stopped and impaled her with his eyes, another thought seeming to have occurred to him. "If I hadn't found out about Anna, would you have told me?"

"Do you mean if you'd never come here?"

"I mean that you've seen me nearly every damned day for the past six weeks. Would I have met her?"

"She was in Florida, at art camp with her best friend."

"How convenient. Would you have let me leave without telling me about her?"

"I don't know." She told him honestly and she could see that he didn't like that answer when he shoved his hand into his hair again.

"You don't know?" His voice rose a few decibels.

"I hadn't decided. I was so shocked when you showed up in the bar. I thought you'd found out somehow. Except that I'd never told anyone. And then you gave me your false name and I knew my secret was still safe. When you first showed interest in me, I caved because I was so curious about you. I wanted to see for myself that my decision had meant something. That you'd made a success of yourself." She smiled at the irony. "And you showed up here impersonating a drug dealer." She took a few cautious steps closer. "But you did, Mike. And I'm glad. I'm so proud of who you've become."

Mike looked around the room and Rachel watched his gaze land on a broken collage frame filled with pictures of Anna spanning from babyhood to her most recent school picture. He looked back at her, his emotions back under control. "So where do we go from here?"

"That's up to you, I guess."

"Did you put my name on her birth certificate?"

"No."

He frowned at that. "Does she know about me?"

"She knows her father is alive in the world somewhere, but she doesn't know it's you. I gave her some mementos of yours I took with me. She treasures them."

Mike looked confused. "What kind of mementos?"

Rachel ducked her head. "A few grainy newspaper photos and the t-shirt I wore home the last time we were together. Your championship ring."

His face immediately cleared. "You still have my ring? I always wondered what happened to it after you left me." Mike began to pace. "I live in D.C."

"I know."

Without a sound Mike was in front of her, tipping her chin up to look into her eyes. "I'd really like to get to know her. I'd like to see the two of you together, how you operate as a family." A tear slipped down Rachel's cheek and he wiped it away with his thumb. "To avoid complicating my case, you'll have to continue to pretend I'm your boyfriend anyway. But while I'm here, I'd love to spend some time with both of you. I have a feeling my dad would, too."

She nodded and another tear fell. "I'm sorry, Rachel. I'd love to do this better. I'd love to step up and *be* her father, but your safety comes first." He wrapped both arms around her waist to pull her tight against him and rested his chin on the top of her head. "It's the best I can do right now."

"It's okay," Rachel mumbled against his neck. "It's more than I expected."

"I still mean what I said on Monday, Rachel. I want to give us a try, long distance or not. Even before

I knew about Anna," he squeezed her, "I knew there was something between us. You know it, too."

She nodded.

Mike loosened his hold and leaned away to look at her. "Go pack a bag for both of you and I'll take you over to my house. I can have my dad take Anna there when they're done. Then I'll call the chief and have him meet me here." He paused to push aside some shards of glass with his toe. "My dad was sure taken with Anna. Imagine what he'll think —" The expression on Rachel's face made him pause.

"He knows," she assured him. "He knew the minute he saw her. I saw him compare the two of you and I could tell he'd worked it out." She groaned as Mike followed her down the hall to her bedroom. "What on earth am I going to tell Anna? She's going to be so confused when you all leave again."

Mike's hand snaked out and spun Rachel on the spot. "We'll work this out. Together this time." He told her firmly.

He righted a chair in the corner and sat down to wait while Rachel sorted through the shambles of her closet and stuffed clothing into a large suitcase before moving on to Anna's room. If he hadn't been watching her so closely she might have sat on the floor and cried. Everything she'd spent nearly a decade building was lying in ruins at her feet.

She threw one last load of toiletries into her case and zipped it shut. Before she'd even bent down to pick it up, Mike was there, suitcase in one hand, the other held out to her. She took his hand, palm to palm, fingers intertwined and they walked out the door together.

Chapter 14

"**A**re you sure we won't be in the way at your place?" Rachel chewed her lip as Mike pulled away from the curb.

"My rental has three bedrooms and two bathrooms, built for a family. There's plenty of room for all of us. If everything goes according to the plan, the sting should take place next week. By then we should have your house put back together."

"Your poor father! He didn't sign on for babysitting two of us." She tried to sound lighthearted, but it fell flat in the face of Mike's hard look. In fact, he said nothing else on the ride over. The silence was scarier to Rachel than listening to his anger and disappointment would have been. His stony expression gave nothing away.

She followed him into the house and set Anna's bag against the wall next to the one that Mike had carried in for her. She had no idea what she was supposed to do or say in a moment like this. In her own house she would have hurried off to clean something. She found comfort in cleaning. The monotony of a good hard scrub was the perfect way to work out problems. But she suspected that Mike wouldn't appreciate it if she started straightening his house.

"So, where do you want us?"

"Excuse me?" He turned to face her and the look on his face made her take a step back. He didn't look angry exactly, more like intensely serious. She wondered what he was thinking about.

"Which bedroom should we take?"

"Oh." He shrugged. "My father is using the room at the back of the house. You can take the one across from mine."

She nodded. He went into his bedroom and shut the door, so Rachel grabbed their bags and started toward the room he'd indicated. She paused in the doorway when she heard the door open again. Mike had changed into jeans and T-shirt and was snapping his gun into his holster. "I'm going to meet the chief at your house. Keep the door locked until my dad gets back with Anna."

Rachel nodded and swallowed hard. "Mike," she called before he left the house. He paused, but he didn't turn around. "For what it's worth, I am sorry I never told you. I was only trying to protect you." She saw his shoulders drop and then he turned around and came back to her. He pulled her into his arms and rested his chin on her head. "I know, baby." He gave her a quick hug, pulled away and went back to the door. "I should be back in a couple of hours."

Gray arrived shortly after with a very excited Anna in tow.

"Mom, guess what? Grandpa," she stopped to point at Gray, in case Rachel had forgotten who she was referring to, "got me a double scoop mint chocolate chip cone dipped in chocolate."

"Wow!" Rachel blinked at her daughter. "And you didn't even get any on you? You must be growing up on me."

Anna beamed and then poked a thumb at Gray. "He made me wear a napkin around my neck."

Rachel nodded at Gray. "Thank you. I do believe you saved a shirt."

Gray gave her an indulgent smile. "I've been known to save a few shirts in my day." He hung up his coat and turned back to her. "So, is everything settled?"

"Settled for now, anyway. We just got here a few minutes ago. Mike went back to meet the police at my house. We're going to stay here with you guys for a few days so I was just getting ready to unpack."

Anna had been wandering around the house and returned to ask, "We're going to stay here? Really?"

"Yes, really." Rachel teased her. "So you're have to keep your tornado-mess tendencies to yourself."

Anna giggled. "This is going to be so much fun! Which room do I get?"

"You're in the first room there, with me."

"No!" She drew the word out to show her disappointment. "I don't want to share a room with you. Why can't I have my own room?"

"Anna Michelle!"

Gray looked up, startled.

"There are three bedrooms and three adults in this house. You will need to share a room with me."

"Why can't you share a room with Mike? Isn't he the man you went on a date with?" She gave her mother a sage look. "People do that, you know."

"Anna." Rachel warned. Her cheeks flushed. Where on earth had Anna heard such a thing?

"Or you can sleep on the couch?"

"Maybe you should sleep on the couch." Rachel quipped. "You're the smallest."

At Gray's guffaw, she narrowed her eyes at her whining daughter. "We'll talk about it later."

Anna stomped to the room Rachel had indicated. Rachel turned back to Gray. "She doesn't understand what she's asking. I promise. I don't even know where she got those ideas from."

Gray smiled. "I know, Rachel. She's a good girl. You've done a great job raising her. I couldn't ask for a better grandchild."

Rachel looked up into his eyes and noted the sincerity there.

"I imagine it must have been hard, raising her alone, but she's simply wonderful."

Rachel nodded, unable to speak around the lump in her throat. His expression softened.

"I'm here if you ever need to talk."

Rachel nodded again and turned to go help Anna unpack the few things they'd brought along. Anna continued to argue her case for having her own room. Rachel was thankful that her daughter was still too innocent to understand why asking her mother to share a room with Mike was a bad idea.

Mike returned to his house just as Rachel was setting the table for dinner. He paused in the entry and took in the cozy scene playing out in front of him. Anna was following her mother around the table adding silverware and napkins as his father stirred something at the stove, and for a moment Mike was overcome with intense longing. This is what was missing in his life, a family to come home to. Just as quickly he realized this was his family. The anger and hurt he'd been carrying for the last several hours left him. He'd been given a chance to know his daughter, and a second chance with Rachel. This time they weren't going to mess it up.

Rachel was the first to notice him standing in the doorway. He gave her a small wink and it hurt him to notice that she didn't maintain eye contact with him for long. He owed her an apology but it would have to wait until they were alone.

"What's for dinner?" He asked in a cheerful voice as he entered the kitchen.

"Spaghetti," Gray answered. "Anna's specialty."

Mike turned to the girl who had his hair, his eyes. "You made dinner?"

She nodded. "I'm a good cook. I've been making stuff for years."

"For years, huh?" He grinned at her confidence. "What else do you know how to cook?" He was entertained by the animated way Anna spoke. She was all hands. He remembered the training he had to undergo at the academy to turn off that particular trait. His daughter had inherited that from him.

"I can make pancakes, mac and cheese, grilled cheese, and soup, but anybody can make that stuff. Spaghetti is what I do best."

"Well, I'm starving, and I can't wait to try it."

Anna beamed at him and then at her mother. Mike looked from Rachel to his daughter and was struck by how beautiful they both were.

Gray and Anna did most of the talking during dinner, which kept the mood light. Mike knew Anna was impervious to the undercurrent of his and Rachel's serious moods, but his father was not. He was intentionally keeping the conversation focused on Anna to give her parents time to adjust to their new reality.

"Oh! Mom, did you talk to Mr. Mike about the bedrooms?"

"Rachel closed her eyes looking like her patience was strained. "No, Anna. I told you that we would talk about it later."

"Just Mike." He reminded Anna. "What's the matter with the bedrooms?"

"Nothing," Rachel answered, with a voice that dared her daughter to contradict her. But Anna wouldn't be derailed.

"I don't want to share a room with my mom. I'm not a baby anymore. I think you should let her share your room with you. I saw your bed. It's huge. Plus, she sleeps really quiet so you won't even know she's there. I know you took her on a *date*." She wiggled her eyebrows.

Rachel groaned and Gray laughed aloud. Mike held his smile but his eyes sought Rachel's. Her blush gave away her embarrassment. "Your mother and I can talk about it later," Mike agreed with a nod. Anna bounced in her seat.

"Yes!" She turned to her mother with a brag in her voice. "See, Mom? I told you it was no big deal."

"We only agreed to talk about it. You can sleep on the couch. and I'll sleep in the extra bedroom," Rachel reminded her in a mom-voice. "Okay, Anna. Shower and bedtime."

Anna groaned. "Oh come on! Why can't I take a shower tomorrow? I want to stay up longer."

"Anna Michelle," she warned. "Don't argue with me. It's been a long day and we're all exhausted. Come on. Hop up." She got Anna settled in the bathroom while Mike cleaned up the kitchen from dinner.

"Anna's middle name is Michelle?" Mike asked when she re-entered the living room after settling Anna in her temporary room to go to sleep. Gray looked up from his book.

"Yes. After Michael, for you. After your mother, Michelle." Rachel blushed as she shared that very personal information. "You told me once your mother's name was Michelle. I wanted her to have some little piece of you, of your side of the family."

When Mike spoke, his voice was rough with emotion. "Do you know my mother passed away just over a year ago? She had breast cancer."

Rachel bowed her head, her heart heavy for a woman that she'd never met. "No. I'm sorry, I had no idea."

Gray stood and placed the paper on the seat behind him. He approached her and pulled her into a tight hug. "It's a beautiful tribute. She would have been moved by your thoughtfulness. I'd like to think she's in heaven, even now, crying over this." He smiled but she could see the tears in his eyes before he left the room.

She wandered closer to the couch where Mike was sitting, his laptop now open on the table in front of him. "Mike, about the sleeping arrangements," she swallowed and then cleared her throat when that didn't help. "Anna doesn't understand what she's asking. She's still innocent to all that."

Mike looked amused. "I kind of thought it was a brilliant tactic. And I don't have any problem with it."

Rachel resisted the urge to roll her eyes. "Of course you don't."

He put his hands on her hips and guided her onto his lap. She instinctively put her arms around his neck when he leaned in to nuzzle behind her ear. "My dad's right. She's a smart girl. It's a win-win solution."

"For you two, maybe," she retorted. Mike laughed. "But the fact is that she's young and to her, you're just a boyfriend. It's not appropriate."

"We'll be discreet." He gave her a quick kiss on the lips and became serious. "We need to talk."

She sneaked a look at his face but it was unreadable. "About the break in?"

"And other things," he confirmed. Her stomach clenched.

"Can I make sure Anna's in bed first?"

He rubbed her shoulders. "Sure."

Rachel went in to check on Anna and found her sound asleep on the bed already. She was surprised, but then, it had been a big day for her from flying alone from Florida, to the break-in, to staying in a strange house. She'd been so brave, taking everything in stride. Rachel tucked the blankets around her and turned on a little lamp next to the bed to give her some light in case she woke before Rachel came to bed. Then she grabbed some pajamas from a drawer and changed her clothes, dragging out the time until they had their talk. Double checking that Anna's clothes were laid out for the next day, she closed the door softly behind her and crossed the hall.

"Mike?" She entered his bedroom cautiously, looking around for him.

"Yes?" He came into the room from the attached master bath with nothing but a towel wrapped around his waist, water still dripping from his inky black hair.

Rachel's throat went dry. She clenched her jaw to keep it from dropping in awe. She'd never get enough of seeing him this way. "You, ah, wanted to talk?"

He quirked an eyebrow at her. "Is Anna asleep?"

"Yes."

"Then yes, but besides that, you're sleeping in here. With me."

"I guess that depends on what you have to say."

Mike gave her a look of exasperation and shook his head. Turning his back on her, he took a pair of soft gray pajama bottoms from a drawer and pulled them on. She glanced away out of modesty and when she looked back he was hanging his towel on the bar in the bathroom.

"I walked through your place with Mobely. He documented the break in and had one of the deputies take prints. They'll have you go through tomorrow and list anything that's missing."

Rachel frowned. "I don't own much of value. My jewelry was still there. My TV and DVD player were destroyed. It wasn't a burglary, Mike."

He sat on the side of the bed and looked up at her. His bare chest was a distraction.

"I have more." His eyes searched her face.

"I'm not sure I can handle anything more tonight."

"I owe you an apology. I was hard on you today. Finding out about Anna shocked me. I showed you my anger at missing out on the first nine years of her life but I didn't appreciate how much you sacrificed to give her a good upbringing. Anna is amazing. And you're amazing for making it through alone. You've got to be the strongest woman I know. On top of that, your involvement in my case has put a target on your back and now your house has been destroyed. Whether or not the break in is even related to my case, I know that you're struggling."

"It has been a hell of a day," she agreed.

He pulled her down onto his lap again. "Shall we end it on a high note then?"

She tipped her face up to his. "What did you have in mind?"

His face brightened. "Let me show you."

Seconds later he'd locked the door and tugged her nightgown up over her head. He pressed her back into the bed and nuzzled her neck as his hands rubbed over her already feverish skin. He skimmed off her panties and positioned himself between her legs and then paused. "I'm really the only man you've ever slept with?"

Rachel opened her eyes and gave him the truth. "You're all I've ever wanted, Mike."

With his heart in his eyes he bent his head to capture her lips in a long, gentle kiss. Her confession clearly affected him, Rachel could feel his emotion as he made love to her.

Long moments later he pulled the sheet over the both of them and settled her against him back to front. With a content sigh, he whispered, "I could stay like this forever."

Rachel smiled and rolled away to lean over the side of the bed. She snatched up his sweatpants and tossed them at his face.

"I could too, but under the circumstances, it would be a good idea to have clothes on in case my daughter comes looking for me before I can sneak back in there."

"Our daughter," he muttered, trying out the phrase.

Rachel pulled on her nightgown and underwear and then settled back in bed to face him as he pulled his pants on.

"She talks with her hands," he commented.

Rachel smiled. "I know. And she's a huge sports fan. She doesn't get that from me."

"Yeah?" He grinned.

"She gets decent grades but I think she spends too much time socializing. She's pretty popular, I think. She has a good heart and she's generous."

His expression softened. "She gets that from you."

"Sometimes she's mouthy."

Mike laughed. "She gets that from you, too."

Rachel punched his shoulder lightly and then rolled over to give him her back. He hauled her up against his chest and threw a leg over both of hers to hold her there. "As I was saying," he repeated, "I could stay like this forever."

"It is rather nice," she agreed, and feeling safe at the end of a long and emotional day, she fell asleep.

Chapter 15

Mike was gone well before dawn the next morning and Rachel was thankful that he'd woken her up in time for her to sneak back into bed beside Anna. She knew Anna was well aware that men and women shared rooms, for nearly all of Anna's friends had fathers, but it had never been a part of their lives. Even the experience of staying with other people was new.

Gray was sitting at the small dining table sipping his coffee when Rachel padded into the kitchen.

"Morning. Did you sleep well?"

"I did." Rachel nodded. "Better than I have in a long time."

"Having your whole life turned on its ear will do that to a person."

She gave a short laugh. "That must be it." She poured a cup of coffee and joined him at the table. "You're up early for a retired guy."

"Left over from my career days. I can't seem to shake the schedule. I did most of my surgeries in the early hours and had office consultations in the afternoon."

"That must have made for some long days." Rachel sympathized.

"After Michelle was diagnosed I found that my heart just wasn't in it anymore." He gave a quick smile over his pun. "So I turned my practice over to an up-and-comer and took to following Mike around the country. It keeps us close and he doesn't seem to mind having me around."

"I'm sure he appreciates it. His job takes a lot out of him. And I remember how close he was to you guys in college."

Gray nodded. "He's a good man."

"He is."

Gray peeked up at her. "How long did you know one another before, ah, Anna came along?"

Rachel felt the blush creeping up her cheeks. It was embarrassing but she felt she owed him an explanation. "We had a couple of classes together. We were assigned on a project together in one of them. We hadn't been dating very long at all." She traced the rim of her coffee cup, unable to meet his eyes.

"If you don't mind my asking, why didn't you tell him you were pregnant?"

She shrugged, putting a brave face on her feelings. "Mike had so much going for him. By the time I knew

I was pregnant the semester was over and we'd both gone home for the summer and I had some serious decisions to make regarding college. I considered looking him up, but ultimately, I decided I would be messing up his life, too. So I kept it to myself."

Gray cut her a level look across the table. "I'll bet he didn't like hearing that."

Rachel almost smiled at the understatement. "No, he didn't."

"Anna said I'm the only grandfather she's ever had. What happened with your family? Weren't they supportive?"

The coffee turned to acid in her stomach. She pushed her cup away. "No." She closed her eyes and swallowed. She hadn't thought about her family in a long time. "My sister is married to a race car driver. I saw on the news not long ago that they had a baby. I'm sure my parents are very excited about that."

"But they weren't excited about your baby, I take it?" He was frowning at her, but she could see the concern in his eyes.

"I was young, barely twenty-three. Single and getting ready to start my residency."

"Med school?" Gray winced. "Your parents couldn't have helped you?"

"My father has a reputation to maintain. He's the CEO of–well, it's a famous company. They are often in the spotlight. My parents pride themselves in their charity work but they don't condone their daughter becoming one of those cases. They demanded to know who the father was, of course. I knew that the minute I gave them Mike's name his life would change–and not for the better. My father would have demanded a quick, quiet marriage and then he would have found a place for Mike in the company. And all of Mike's aspirations might have led to nothing." She swiped at a tear. "I couldn't do that to him." She gave a watery laugh. "I couldn't even do that to myself. When they gave me an ultimatum, I left."

Gray sat back. "You must have loved Mike an awful lot."

Rachel drew her brows together. "What makes you say that?"

"That's a hell of a sacrifice for a stranger."

He pursed his lips and then continued his questioning. She knew where Mike got it. "So your family didn't support you and you took off."

"I didn't feel like I really had a choice." She looked at Gray with a mixture of pride and sadness. "There have been some hard times, but I've never once sacrificed my dignity."

He acknowledged that with a nod. "It doesn't amount to much now, but we would have been there for you, Michelle and I. We would have accepted the situation for what it was and welcomed you and Anna into our family in whatever capacity you'd have us fill." He flashed a quick smile. "Probably even without a shot-gun wedding. I still will."

Tears ran down Rachel's face as she swallowed back the sick feeling of regret for having cheated them out of that chance. "At the time I had no way of knowing that. But I believe you." She brushed away the fresh tears and attempted a smile. "You're here now."

He placed a hand over hers. "And it's been one of the highlights of my life."

They heard Anna stirring so Rachel wiped her face and got up to warm her coffee. They both laughed when she automatically filled Gray's cup as well. "Once a waitress, always a waitress," she teased. But Gray didn't smile. They both knew that she would have been a doctor.

"Grandpa!"

Anna's delighted greeting brought a smile to both of their faces.

"You're still here."

"This is where I live for now, silly goose."

"This is so cool!" Anna told her mom as Rachel set a bowl of cereal in front of her. "Mom, can we stay here, too? Like even after our house is fixed?"

Rachel's smile slid from her face. "No, honey. This is Mike's house. Soon we'll need to go back to our own house." Rachel's reminder seemed to cast a gloom in the kitchen.

After breakfast Rachel urged Anna to hurry and get dressed so they could go school shopping.

"Can Grandpa take me? It'll save you a trip." Anna looked hopeful but Rachel knew better. She wanted to show off her new relative.

When Rachel looked at Gray and saw that his expression matched Anna's, she caved. "Oh, all right! But don't get used to it," she warned as Anna ran back to her room to grab her list.

"Save the receipts and I'll write you a check when you get back."

"Rachel, let me do this. I know that you can take care of her, but this is new to me. I won't spoil her, I promise."

Rachel studied him for a moment, fighting her instinct to refuse the help. "Okay. But I mean it—stick with what's on the list. She'll hammer you for everything and she just doesn't need it."

Gray grinned, looking exactly like Mike did when he got his way.

Anna was back with the little pack she liked to carry as a purse, waving her school list around. "Ready!"

Rachel pulled her into a hug and then gave her the customary warning. "I'm telling you the same thing I told your grandpa. Stick with what's on the list. Nothing more. Do you remember your sizes?"

"Yes, Mom."

"Great. Make sure you leave room in your clothes to grow. Shoes, too."

"I know, Mom."

Gray looked at her for a moment. "Mike left this key for you."

"Thanks."

"Rachel?"

She looked from the key to his face.

"Thank you."

She nodded feeling the weight of his gratitude, gave them one last warning look and then waved them away. Having the day free now meant that she could start putting her house back together so she threw on a tank and shorts and gave Savannah a call to let her know she wouldn't be in to work that day.

Chapter 16

Starting in the kitchen because it had the least amount of overturned furniture to work around, Rachel settled herself on the floor to begin the tedious task of sorting her belongings back into their drawers and cupboards. She believed in keeping an attitude of thankfulness, so she gave thanks for the fact that she didn't own much, which meant there was less to wash and put away. As she worked, she made a list for her insurance company of the things that would need to be replaced.

Not much later she heard the front door open and assumed it was Mike, returning from his meeting with Bill and his team. "In the kitchen," she called to let him know she was there.

"Oh, good Lord!" Savannah's voice issued from the doorway. "What the heck did you get yourself into, Rachel?"

Rachel scrambled to her feet, surprised to see Savannah and Daniel looking around at the mess with concern. She plunked her hands on her hips. "Why must you assume I brought this upon myself?" Rachel asked. She knew Savannah well enough not to be offended by her question.

Savannah pushed a pile of canned food toward Rachel with her toe. "Oh, I don't know. Maybe it's your new taste in men?"

Rachel knew that Savannah was only speaking out of concern, but Daniel surprised them both with his angry, "Savannah!"

From the living room, another voice added, "I'm not all that bad once you get to know me."

Daniel and Savannah whirled around as Mike entered the kitchen behind them. Rachel wanted to run to him, to let him hold her, but for the sake of appearances, she kept her ground.

Mike's face relaxed into a smile as he greeted Daniel. "Hey buddy." They embraced with a one-armed whack to each other's backs before Mike moved to stand next to Rachel, settling a possessive arm around her waist.

Both women looked back and forth. Rachel in confusion, Savannah with consternation.

Savannah was the first to speak. "What the hell's going on around here?"

Rachel snorted. "I was just thinking the same thing."

Daniel and Mike smiled at each other, clearly enjoying some private joke. Daniel spoke first.

"Savannah, this is Mike Renner. My roommate from college."

"Mike, this is my fiancée, Savannah Decatur."

Mike reached out to shake her hand. Rachel held onto her smile as Savannah's eyes grew round. "Oh my," she said to Rachel.

"It's nice to officially meet you. I was sorry to miss the museum's grand opening. I was detained in Detroit at the time."

Savannah smiled at Mike and then whirled back to her fiancé. "Why didn't you just tell me he wasn't a bad guy? I would've been nicer to him."

Daniel gave her an exasperated sigh. "That's the point. You're not supposed to be nice to him. Everyone to believe he is a bad guy."

"Okay. But all this time I've been harping on poor Rachel about him. I told her to stay away from him. I considered kidnapping her to keep her away."

"Did you really?" Rachel asked, humbled by how much her friend cared.

"I was worried about you! I am so sorry, Rach."

Rachel reached out to pull Savannah in for a hug. "It's okay, really. I knew where your motives were."

"How did you know he wasn't really a bad guy?"

Rachel looked at Mike, not sure how to respond. He answered for her.

"We knew each other back in college. She remembered me right away."

Daniel squinted at Mike and then his eyes popped over to Rachel. "No way. Really? Rachel's that Rachel?"

Rachel saw Savannah look back and forth with great interest and then noticed the sparkle in Mike's eyes. She turned her gaze to the floor, shaking her head. She knew what was coming next.

"The one and only. And I'm Anna's father."

Savannah patted her chest. "I need to sit down." Daniel righted a chair for her and leaned back against the countertop while Mike turned the topic to the break in.

"My dad's staying at my rental with Rachel and Anna while I go back to D.C. I have a few more days of testimony and then I'll be closing up the case her in Wolf Creek."

Savannah cocked her head. "Who are you?" The look in her eyes indicated that she was half teasing, but Rachel took pity on her.

"He's undercover for the DEA. He's looking into Big Jim's racket." Rachel implored Savannah with her eyes. "You absolutely cannot tell anyone. And you've got to keep treating him like you think he's a rat."

Savannah laughed. "How am I supposed to treat him like a rat when I know he's your long lost love?"

"Savannah, I'm serious. You absolutely cannot talk about this."

Savannah made the sign of a cross over her heart. "Okay. I promise."

"What's the plan?" Daniel wanted to know.

The two men went from room to room setting the furniture back in place while Mike took Daniel through the next steps of the operation.

Savannah followed Rachel around, helping her put the smaller things back in their places. "Does Anna know about her father?"

"Anna knows her father is out there somewhere. She has a few pictures of Mike that I cut out of the college paper when he was playing hockey, and a few things of his that I'd kept. She met Mike yesterday. But she doesn't know he's her father."

"Are you going to tell her?"

"Eventually, yes. We haven't really talked about it yet, but I know Mike will want to stay in her life now that he knows about her."

Savannah's jaw dropped. "He didn't know?"

"I never told anybody. Not even Mike."

"Oh Rachel!" Savannah yanked Rachel forward and squeezed her hard. "You are so brave."

"I don't know about that, but now that they've met, there's no going back." Rachel removed the broken glass from a framed picture and hung the picture back on the wall. "The family friend that's here to visit me is Mike dad. He's really here to watch over me until the case is wrapped up. Mike's worried there will be danger."

"I had no idea. I wonder why he didn't ask Daniel?"

"Knowing Mike, he probably thought Daniel wouldn't be safe if their connection was revealed."

"What does Anna think of all this?"

Rachel thought of Anna's insistence on Gray taking her shopping and gave Savannah a huge smile. "She's in love with Mike's dad and Gray is totally taken with her as well. He asked her to call him grandpa yesterday and she never even questioned it. They're like two peas in a pod already. He even took her school shopping today."

Savannah watched Rachel with a hesitant look.

"What's the matter?"

"How is she going to handle it when they leave?"

Rachel stopped sweeping and leaned on the broom. She looked around to be sure they were alone. "Mike lives in Washington D.C. He'd like to try a long-distance relationship. We decided on that even before he found out about Anna."

Savannah stood to drop a load of glass into the trash bin and then tilted her head at Rachel and lowered her voice. "For what it's worth, Rach, I'm proud of you. Anna is a wonderful girl. You know I love her like she was my own niece."

Rachel nodded. "Thank you."

Between the four of them they managed to get the house put back together in no time. There were a lot of things that Rachel would have to replace, some of which had meaning to her but she reminded herself that she and Anna were okay, and that was what truly mattered.

Chapter 17

Sending Mike back to D.C. on Monday morning seemed infinitely harder after such an emotional weekend. Rachel got up early with Mike to enjoy a few minutes of time alone with him before he had to leave. Despite the streak of independence she'd always prided herself on, she followed Mike around the house like a pet being left behind as he gathered his things.

Mike dropped his carry-on suitcase and beat up old backpack by the door and then turned and gave Rachel a playful pout. He pulled her forward against his chest and linked his arms around her lower back.

Rachel cuddled in close and sighed. Mike tipped her face up for a kiss and said, "I'll be back by the weekend and I'll call you later."

"I know," Rachel mumbled. She straightened away and rubbed her eyes. "I'm being silly and emotional. I'm used to being alone." Her shoulders sagged a little as she looked up into his eyes. "Having you around is just too easy to get used to."

Mike made a sound like a painful groan and yanked her back against his chest. "We'll work this out, baby. But right now, I've got a plane to catch."

With one last very thorough kiss, Mike grabbed his bags and bolted out to his car. Rachel leaned against the doorjamb and watched until Mike's car could no longer be seen.

Once Anna and Gray were awake, Rachel's attention was redirected to more domestic matters. She helped prepare breakfast and cleaned up afterward and then updated her work schedules in a calendar that Gray had attached to the refrigerator. Then she left Anna with him and headed over to her house to collect her mail. She let herself in to make sure everything was secure. On the table was the largest check she'd received since leaving the affluent lifestyle of her parents behind. It was the payment from her insurance adjuster to replace the furniture and other items that had been destroyed in the break-in. Rachel tucked it carefully in her purse and looked around at how much still needed to be done.

She could leave Mike's house and come home, she knew. They had enough to be get by. But a louder voice in her mind seduced her with two very potent reminders. Anna was getting the opportunity to get to know her grandfather, and for the time being, Rachel and Anna weren't alone.

Rachel went into the kitchen to see if she had anything to take to Mike's house to cook for dinner later. She searched through several cupboards as well as the refrigerator and freezer. She knew Gray was a healthy eater but what she found wouldn't be enough to sustain three people.

She hated to think how she would pay for it later and maybe she'd have to use some of the insurance money, but for now she had a credit card and she knew that buying groceries would let her feel like she was contributing so she snatched up her keys and purse and headed to Pat's Grocery.

She grabbed a cart and strolled up and down the aisles, giving thought to what they could cook for the week. It turned out to be an interesting exercise, deciding which healthy meals Gray would like that Anna would also eat without too much complaint, and figuring out how much to buy. She'd never cooked for a man, let alone a family of three, so she bought a little extra of everything.

Rachel felt self-conscious as she wheeled up to the cashier and unloaded the cart onto the conveyor. She never bought this much, and being a regular customer, the cashier probably knew it. Rachel tried not to sweat as the total climbed. She'd called the customer service number on the back of her card to be sure the charge would go through, but she was nervous anyway. It was unlike her to spend money without any idea of how she'd pay for it. It was yet another support beam crashing around her carefully structured life.

The cashier was feeling chatty and Rachel ground her teeth as the woman carried on a one-sided conversation.

"I heard Tilly hasn't shown up for work in a few days. What do you 'spose happened to her? First that Jay guy and now Tilly. That's two people that just up and left. I swear there's something going on around here. Is Suds a bad place to work, or what?"

The nervous feeling in the pit of Rachel's stomach intensified at the mention of Tilly's name. She wasn't about to comment on Tilly's absence, but Rachel felt it strongly.

"And then poor Carl got beat up a week or so ago! Did he ever say what happened?"

Yeah, Rachel thought, he met the end of my boyfriend's fist, but aloud she said, "No."

"Hmm. And then I heard you been seeing a new guy in town. I seen him around a time or two. Looks kinda shady. I seen Tilly hanging all over him at the bar awhile back. Is that awkward?" She held out a hand to placate Rachel in case she was inclined to answer the questions being fired at her. "He's hot–don't get me wrong. I totally get what you see in him. But don't you think he's probably on the wrong side of the law? I mean, it don't seem like you'd date a guy like that." She didn't give Rachel a chance to answer that either. "And you have a little girl, right? He don't strike me as the fatherly type."

Rachel almost smiled. Oh, how she wished she could set the woman straight, in both her grammar and her information.

"I guess you never know about people, right?" The cashier commented mostly to herself.

Rachel nodded, trying to swallow as she saw the total for the groceries. She held her breath and swiped the card through the machine. The five or so seconds it took before the approval popped up on the screen felt like long minutes. She hoped her face didn't show the relief she felt as she took the receipt from the cashier.

"You be careful, okay? That guy you're with, he could be bad news."

Rachel blinked at the woman. They weren't even on a first-name basis and now her parenting skills were available for questioning. "Uh, thanks." Rachel tried to add a smile, but she wasn't sure she'd pulled it off.

People were buying Mike's act, and Rachel was sure he'd be pleased to know that. But, as she'd reminded him several times, she still had to live in this town after he left. She sighed. The best she could hope for was that people would know he was a good guy before he left so that her reputation wouldn't be permanently destroyed.

The DEA could make their arrests within the week and then he'd leave. With him would go Gray. How would Anna react to going back to their poor, solitary existence? She had no doubt that Mike and Gray would keep in touch now that they knew about Anna, but they both lived too far away to satisfy a nine-year-old's need for family.

Rachel's stomach twisted as she wondered how she could live, seeing Mike only on occasional weekends or holidays. They had something good between them right now, while they were together. But she didn't fool herself. She wasn't a catch for a man like Mike, and she knew that once he was finished in Wolf Creek and moved on to bigger and better things, he could be finished with her as well. Rachel's heart cracked when she realized that since he would be a part of Anna's life, Rachel would know when he fell in love and married one day. And oh, how that would kill her!

Gray was in the kitchen when Rachel returned with the groceries so he helped her carry in the bags and put things away. "This must have cost a fortune!" He commented as he packed some of the meat into the freezer.

"An arm and a leg," she muttered. When he smiled, she added, "And then I almost lost my other arm to the cashier."

At his confused look, she explained, "I almost had to chew it off to get out of there."

He chuckled. "That bad, huh?"

She shook her head in wonder. "Suddenly even people I don't even know are seeing fit to warn me off about Mike. I had no idea I was so popular around here."

He watched her, his expression solemn. "You've made an impression on people. They care enough to worry."

She acknowledged that. "Some of them, anyway. Some just want gossip."

"You can't please everyone."

Chapter 18

The cashier's casual reference to Tilly's M.I.A. status stuck with Rachel until Friday afternoon, when on a whim, she decided to drive by Tilly's place. Parking near the door, Rachel twirled her keyring around her index finger and climbed the stairs to Tilly's second story apartment. She saw the notice on the door before she'd taken more than five steps. Tilly was being evicted.

Rachel's insides seemed to shrink. Tilly was occasionally irresponsible about her schedule and frequently irresponsible about the men she dated, but Rachel knew how much she loved her apartment and even her job. No way would she have blown off both. How long had she been having money troubles? Why hadn't she simply asked for help? Where was she? Rachel banged on the door and waited but there was no answer.

Feeling creeped out and very much in uncharted territory with the situation, Rachel hurried to her car and locked her doors as soon as she was inside. She pulled out her phone and dialed Tilly again. Still no answer. She texted Mike. For more than a week she'd managed to convince herself that Tilly was simply off on one of her boyfriend-benders. But no more. Something bad had happened to her friend. Tears came to Rachel's eyes as she came to terms with the idea. When Mike didn't text back right away, she assumed he was still in court, and headed home. She was taking Tilly's closing shift tonight and wanted to spend some time with Anna before her long and miserable evening dodging wandering eyes and hands.

Being fully familiar with Rachel's schedule, Gray had a light dinner laid out for Rachel when she got there. She gave him a grateful smile and sat down with he and Anna to eat.

"What did you do this afternoon?" Rachel asked her daughter, knowing Anna would be the perfect diversion for her wayward thoughts.

"I used my skills today." Anna showed her several pieces of art she'd done that day, going into detail about the colors and meaning and even described the techniques she'd used.

"This is amazing, Anna. Wow. We'll have to get some frames so we can display these." Quick, hot tears built up behind her eyes as she thought about how quickly Anna was growing up. She caught herself before she sighed aloud. It wasn't like her to be so emotional.

Checking again for a response from Mike, Rachel laid her phone down and bent to kiss Anna's forehead.

"I've got to change for work, sweetie. Be good for Grandpa tonight."

Gray trailed Rachel as far as her bedroom door. "What's wrong?"

Rachel tried to fend off the dread but even her hands were shaking. Saying it aloud couldn't make it true, she could tell Gray her worry. "I'm afraid something really bad has happened to my co-worker. My friend."

"Have you called the police?"

She shook her head. "No. Not yet. She's involved in the case so I texted Mike, but I haven't heard back yet."

Gray gave her should a reassuring squeeze. "It's almost the end of the day. He should be wrapped up in D.C. soon."

Rachel nodded. "I hope so."

"Call the police as a concerned friend. It can't hurt."

With lightning speed, Rachel changed into the white button-up blouse and black skirt that served as her uniform, fumbling with the buttons. She kissed Anna one more time, threw Gray a wave and hurried out the door.

On the way to the bar, she dialed the non-emergency line to the police station and explained her concerns to Shari, the operator on call. Feeling that she'd done what she could for now, Rachel turned her mind to the evening ahead. She hated working the night shift and hated even more working Jim's private parties.

She dreaded it more than usual tonight. For weeks now she'd been under Mike's watchful protection. She hadn't been on anyone's radar apart from Carl's occasional jealousy over her new relationship status. Now, she would have to work the party knowing that if things got out of hand there was no one there to protect her. Irrationally, the realization that she'd allowed herself to lean on Mike to the point of needing him now made her angry. She had depended only on herself her entire adult life and so very quickly it seemed, she'd grown weak.

Rachel clocked in and pulled an apron from the hook. Checking her watch, she estimated she had enough time to circle the dining room and check on the dinner crowd before she'd need to be in the back room to start filling drink orders.

She greeted several of her regulars and refilled their drinks before she recognized a group of local thugs making their way to the bar. Showtime.

Rachel waited near the door of the back room as men seated themselves around a U-shaped banquet table. Following protocol, she waited until Jim was seated before moving forward to place his drink in front of him, then immediately did the same for Carl.

The next hour had her hopping filling drinks, taking dinner orders, delivering food, and filling more drinks until Big Jim raised a beefy hand for silence. He looked like Mafia Santa, right here in Wolf Creek. Rachel was on the verge of excusing herself to the kitchen for a break when Jim's opening statement froze her mid-step.

"This is the big leagues, boys. Ricky Jimienez is coming up in a couple of days. I don't want to see any of the petty fighting over street corners bull I've seen in the past. You're entrepreneurs. We're going to show the man that Wolf Creek may be small, but we're not hicks."

Rachel searched around the room for an empty glass or a plate to clear. Dammit! Why did she have to be so efficient tonight? She normally left when Jim or Carl started the meeting, but whatever Jim was about to say would surely have bearing on Mike's case. Frustrated but with no plausible reason to stay, Rachel was forced to slide out of the room. Even so, she dragged her feet. She made it no more than ten steps down the dim hall toward the kitchen before Carl's angry voice hissed in her ear.

"Off to call your boyfriend? Why isn't the big shot here tonight?"

Rachel steeled herself and thought quickly as she spun to face him. "He left town."

"That don't mean you're not still talkin' to him."

"There's nothing here for a man like Mike," Rachel told Carl. And she meant it.

Acting as if Carl looming over her in a dark hallway didn't scare the daylights out of her, she faked a look of disdain and marched into the bright light and relative safety of the kitchen. There, she waited a few minutes to be sure Carl was gone and then hurried into the ladies room to send Mike a text with what she'd overheard.

On a hunch, Rachel sent another text telling Mike to ignore the babble she would send through next. She deleted the thread with the information on Jimienez and started a new one with a string of rambling, desperate attempts to get Mike to come back to Wolf Creek for her. It was pathetic and she nearly groaned, ashamed at how easily the words came to her, but she wouldn't put it past any of Jim's thugs to snoop through her texts.

Rachel tucked her phone back into her purse and went back to the door of the private dining room to see if Jim had finished his speech. She peered around to see whether anyone needed a drink refill and then leaned against the wall outside the door. Big Jim droned on and on but spoke of nothing that Rachel felt was worthy of reporting to Mike, so she allowed her mind to wander until Tiny sidled up next to her.

"When does Anna start school again?" Tiny wanted to know.

"Monday," Rachel replied, keeping one ear on the flow of conversation in the next room. "She's actually looking forward to it."

Tiny smiled. "Of course she is. She's a social little creature. Besides, she had an exciting summer. I'm sure she's just dying to share the details with her girlfriends."

Rachel smiled. Tiny was more right than he knew. It wasn't every summer that a nine-year-old got to spend weeks at art camp and gain a grandfather. She could just imagine Anna telling her friends all about it.

If Jim's tip about Ricky Jimienez turned out to be true, Mike's case could be over as quickly as he planned. It had been so nice, being able to count on Gray to be there when Rachel had to work. Once they left, she'd be right back to coordinating her schedule with school and looking for sitters after school.

"I'm sure she is," Rachel answered, distracted. With a jolt, Rachel realized that Big Jim had finally stopped speaking in his politician voice which meant that the meeting part of the evening was over. The party had begun. Or, it would begin once she'd delivered the next round of drinks.

"Big Jim's done. I've gotta get back in there," Rachel told Tiny with a quick pat on his arm.

"You give that little girl a hug for me. I miss her something terrible."

Rachel leaned in for a hug. "I'll bring her in soon. She'd love to tell you all about camp."

Two hours later she was skirting Jim's drunk guests and wondering how long it would be before she could make her escape into the crush of bar drinkers where at least other women would be there to distract the men. Within the hour, Rachel was able to convince Jim's guys that the bar had better offerings, and they'd wandered, or in some cases, stumbled their way back to the front of the building.

Rachel trailed the last guy out of the room and made a quick stop to drop off a tray of dishes in the kitchen. "Meeting's over, Tiny. I brought you the last of the dishes." She called out knowing that Tiny would be free to leave once the dinnerware had been washed. She headed out onto the floor to see if the wait staff needed any help.

"Oh!" Four steps past the kitchen door, Rachel stopped short feeling shock and a touch of something much more painful. Mike was there at the bar, sitting at on corner stool holding court like a king. With a woman on his lap.

She stared just long enough to convince herself it really was him, collected herself and then dropped her gaze hastily as his head turned her way. Her hands were shaky and she realized she was holding her breath. She blew out a slow breath and snaked through the tables to put some distance between them. She hadn't known he would be here tonight so she didn't know what his angle was, but she hoped she was doing the right thing by staying out of his way.

Convincing herself that he was merely playing a role was a nearly impossible job with a young inebriated brunette wiggling on his lap. She reminded herself over and over that he'd told her he wanted a relationship with her. He had a child with her. Still, her subconscious came up with counter-excuses like "He's never given you any indication that he loves you", or "You don't fit in his life." She went about her job, glad for once, of the many years' experience that allowed her to operate on autopilot because she was sure she wouldn't have been able to concentrate on anything except what Mike was doing in town early.

Unfortunately, Mike's seat was closest to the bar's narrow entrance which meant that Rachel had to squeeze past him each time she needed to pick up an order from Tony, the bartender on duty. She felt Mike's hand brush her arm or her behind as she scooted past the giggling woman on his lap. She couldn't bring herself to look in his eyes, so she pretended he was any other drunk, though she would have bet money that he hadn't had more than a single beer.

On one trip to the bar, Carl waylaid her with a tight fist on the soft flesh just above her elbow. "Lover-boy's back, but it looks like he really has moved on."

Rachel gave him a look that suggested he was stupid. "You really thought he'd stick around for a woman like me?"

"I bet that's not sitting so well, huh?"

"What makes you think so?"

"Just a hunch. I know you, Rachel. And I see the way you look at him. You think you love him. But you know what? Men like that don't love women. They use them and move on. You're just a notch in his belt, sweetheart." He looked down at her with something like bitterness. "I would have been good to you."

She looked at him in disbelief. "You would have been faithful? Taken Anna in?" She shook her head. "I'm sorry, but you're hardly daddy material, Carl."

Carl's eyes narrowed. "And you're looking for a daddy to play happy family with, is that right? Well, you can put your hopes away. You're drowning him with your desperation and every man in the bar can see it. He's moved on. Get out there and do your job. And stop putting designs on my customers."

Rachel looked at Carl, working to conceal her horror at his parting comments. She steadfastly avoided looking at Mike tonight. But before tonight? She wasn't sure she'd been so careful.

With a look that felt a little too knowing, Carl moved in closer making Rachel's skin crawl. "You still want to get Black's attention?"

Rachel half glanced at Mike and then snapped back to Carl.

"Show him you've moved on, too." He whispered near her ear.

Rachel let her disdain show in her expression. "With you? No, thank you."

Carl's face twisted, his expression so dark that Rachel took an involuntary step back and accidentally trod on someone's foot. Almost thankful for the excuse, she turned to apologize to whomever she'd hurt. An older man in his mid-fifties, was standing so closely behind her that he could have wrapped his arms around her waist had he had the urge. Mortified, she wondered how much of their badly concealed conversation he'd heard. Examining him quickly, Rachel decided that he appeared neither violent nor drunk. In fact, there was a twinkle in his eye that she would have found endearing if she wasn't so humiliated.

"I'm so sorry, sir. I hope I didn't hurt you."

His smile felt too personal for a stranger. "How about you dance with me so I can test out my foot. You know, see if it still works and all that."

Rachel blinked at him. As pick-up lines went, his was pretty cliché. But there was something almost insistent in his expression and the alternative was going another round with Carl. She chanced a look at Mike and saw that he was watching her intently. Unable to read his expression, she decided that the stranger was safer than Carl and accepted his offer with a grateful smile. He took her elbow and directed her onto the dance floor and away from Carl.

The music switched to something slow just as they reached the dance floor but instead of bringing Rachel in close, the man offered his left hand and placed his right just above her hip. It was such a gentlemanly action, and so unexpected, that Rachel looked up at him in puzzlement.

"Have we met?" She asked him.

"Not yet," he answered, still looking like he was enjoying a good joke. "You have to be Rachel Henige."

Rachel slowed nearly to a stop. "I am. But we haven't met?" The twinkle spread into a full-blown smile. "Gary Sellers. It's nice to finally meet you."

She reached back in her memory and came up with where she'd heard that name before. With a sigh, she collapsed against him, feeling safer already. "Mike's partner," she whispered near his ear.

"You got it."

They moved silently to the song until it ended. She wasn't sure why Gary was there, or how she should treat him, so she let him lead by example. As soon as the song was over, Gary leaned in as if to thank her for the dance, but instead he asked, "What time do you get off work?"

She glanced at the enormous digital clock above the bar. "Another half hour."

"I'm taking you home tonight. I'll wait for you by the back door in a dark red Chevy."

"Thanks," Rachel told him from the heart. Knowing that Gary was there to see her home safely make Rachel feel a little warmer toward Mike, even though the giggly woman hadn't yet removed her backside from his lap. Rachel chanced another look his way and found herself impaled by his dark eyes. She gave an almost imperceptible nod to let him know that she was fine and then turned back to make sure none of her patrons needed anything before closing out her tabs and preparing to clock out for the night.

When she finally stepped outside, she breathed in the night air. The silence of the night was always a shock to her nerves after the lights and teeth-jarring volume of the music. She stood under the dingy light above the door and felt her nerves jingle as she acclimated herself to the stillness that surrounded her.

A few moments later, a firm hand gripped her elbow, startling her.

"Your ride is waiting. Let's get out of here."

"Oh!" She slapped a hand to her chest, and then released her breath when she realized it was Gary. "Good. I'm ready to go."

He ushered her to his dark red sedan, and waited until she was seated in the passenger seat before hurrying around to get in.

Gary barely had the car started before Rachel began her questions.

"When did you guys get in? And why are you here? Why didn't Mike tell me he was coming back tonight?"

Gary leveled her a look in the dim light of the dash. "I ought to let you do the interrogating. Sheesh!"

Rachel sat back in her seat with a light laugh. "Sorry."

"Well, I can tell you it was later than Mike wanted it to be. I've never known him to be so homesick."

Rachel's heart did a little dance. Mike had been homesick?

His voice sounding all business now, Gary changed the subject. "Mike forwarded me your messages. I'm sorry to hear that he dumped you," he added with a laugh.

Rachel was glad he couldn't see her red face. She'd smack him for that later.

"Tell me everything Jim Charles said about Ricky Jimienez."

Rachel thought back to a few hours earlier and tried to remember what Jim had said. She repeated everything she could think of and once she'd finished, the questions started. Gary stopped questioning her long enough to walk her to the door of Mike's house and then waited in the living room while she checked on Anna and let Gray know she was home.

As soon as she took a seat on the couch, Gary started up again, this time taking notes. It was nearly one a.m. and Rachel was exhausted. She knew, though, that there was no way she'd fall asleep before Mike got there.

Rachel sat and watched Gary update a computer file while she waited for Mike. After a while, Gary looked at her.

"What made you think Mike was homesick?" Rachel asked quietly.

"He said so."

"He told you he was homesick? Meaning he missed Wolf Creek?"

"Well, you guys anyway. I can't wait to meet this little girl of yours. She must be something else, the way he talks about her!"

Rachel cocked her head, surprise jolting her. "He told you about Anna?"

"Went on and on like any proud daddy."

"Huh." Rachel wasn't sure how she felt about that. She was still getting used to the idea of sharing Anna with another person. Pretty soon, it seemed, everyone would know except Anna. Since her relationship with Mike was so new, she didn't know how to respond. "She is pretty amazing."

Gary looked up from his screen and grinned at her. "With parents like hers? How could she not be?" He went back to typing. "Pamela–that's my wife–and I, we never could have kids. She just adopts animals instead."

Rachel smiled, remembering Mike's description of them. "And Mike."

Gary nodded. "And Mike." He snorted. "Though for the record, I am not old enough to be his father."

They were laughing together when Mike came home. He locked the door behind him and strode into the living room. Without a word, he pulled Rachel into his arms and kissed the breath out of her.

Gary cleared his throat. "Plenty of time for that later, Renner," Gary teased.

Reluctantly, Mike set Rachel down and pulled her down next to him on the couch. "What have you got for me?"

Gary went over the notes he'd taken after his conversation with Rachel as well as some things he'd heard at the bar. As the voices droned on, Rachel felt herself drifting off and excused herself to get ready for bed. It was nearly morning and she knew Anna would be up in a few hours.

Rachel quietly closed the bedroom door and headed straight for the shower in the adjoining bathroom. No matter how exhausted she was, she always felt compelled to wash the bar from her skin. She had her face turned up into the hot spray when two strong arms surrounded her and moved up to cup her breasts causing her to jump. Wiping the water from her eyes she looked over her shoulder.

"How did you get in here without making any noise?" Rachel asked Mike as he brushed his hands up and down her sides.

He nibbled on her earlobe, adding to the goosebumps his touch had caused. "Just call me the shower ninja. God, I missed you."

Relaxing back against his chest, Rachel smiled. "I missed you, too."

They made love in the shower until the water ran cold and then they hurried to get dried off in order to rush back to bed. It was dawn by the time Rachel finally fell asleep beside Anna in the spare bedroom.

Chapter 19

Rachel didn't wake until eleven a.m. when an unfamiliar sound jolted her up in bed. She pulled on a zip-up sweatshirt over her tank and cotton shorts and trudged out to the kitchen to see what the commotion was about. Gray was in the living room reading a novel and Anna was at the kitchen table, her school supplies spread across the table. She was packing her backpack for school.

"Mom! Grandpa and I ran out for donuts this morning so that you could sleep in and we saw a sign at the grocery store. Guess what I signed up for today?"

"What's that, sweetheart?" Rachel had started a pot of coffee and now turned around to look at her.

"Hockey tryouts!"

"Really?" Rachel's heart sank. Hockey equipment was expensive. Definitely outside of her budget.

Gray gave up the pretense of not listening and came into the kitchen.

Anna's face glowed with her excitement. "They're having tryouts Tuesday night and I signed up. It's okay if you have to work because Grandpa could take me," her eyes moved from Rachel to Gray. "Right?"

Their eyes locked above Anna's head. She could see how badly he wanted to support Anna in this, and yet he was leaving the decision up to her. She looked back at Anna's hopeful face. It was only tryouts after all. She didn't skate much so there was a good chance she wouldn't even make the team.

"Okay, sweetie. I don't have to work so we'll both go and watch you."

"Yay!" She gave a little hop and twirled and then turned back to her mother. In a stage whisper she asked, "Can I tell him about my daddy?"

Rachel's breath hitched in her throat and she willed herself not to blush. "Uh, I guess so."

Anna turned back to Gray and pulled a necklace from under her sweatshirt. "My daddy played hockey. See?" She held out Mike's championship ring. "This belonged to him."

Gray leaned in to look. "Wow. Well, I can tell you that this is very valuable."

"You've been wearing it?" Rachel asked.

"I was afraid something would happen to it. You know, because the house was broken into."

Anna's fist closed around it and she turned back to Gray. "I take very good care of it. Maybe someday I'll meet him and he might want it back."

Gray's startled eyes met Rachel's. "What do you know about your daddy, if you don't mind my asking?"

Anna looked at her mother, and seeing her nod, she continued. "He was a great hockey player. I look like him. He's a good guy but he lives really far away so I can't go see him."

Gray nodded. "That's a lot. Do you know his name?"

"No. Mom said she'd tell me when I'm old enough to meet him. She said he's really busy but that maybe one day we'd travel out to see him."

"I'm sure that's true," Gray commented. "He sounds like a nice guy."

Anna surprised them both by disagreeing. "I don't think he's all that nice."

"Why not?" Rachel asked. She'd had no idea Anna felt anything other than a fantasy love for her father.

"He didn't want to keep my mom," she told Gray. "Everyone thinks she's really nice and she's really pretty. So he couldn't have been that nice."

Rachel's face heated and she couldn't bring herself to look at Gray.

"You know, Anna? You might be right. Or, maybe he's a good guy but not very smart."

Rachel could hear the laughter in his voice and risked a small smile. Gray winked at her and continued, "Maybe you can tell Mike about your daddy when he gets back."

Rachel gasped but Anna was so intrigued by the idea that she didn't notice her mom's reaction. She squinted up at her grandpa. "You think he'd want to hear about him?"

"I know he would. And you never know, he might even agree with you that your daddy wasn't very smart to let your mom go."

Rachel huffed. "That might be going a little too far."

Gray laughed. She suspected Gray's sense of humor might be a little more forgiving than Mike's. Especially in this.

"Anna, Mike has a lot going on right now. Let's not bother him with silly stuff."

Anna started to disagree, so Rachel made her mom-face. "Okay, reading time! School starts in two days."

Anna groaned and Gray went back to the living room whistling. Rachel went back into the bedroom to get dressed and found a note from Mike on the pillow next to hers. He and Gary would be tied up most of the day working with the chief and the local branch of the FBI to get the sting set up again.

Rachel spent the day doing laundry and helping Anna choose what she would wear on the first day of school. After dinner that evening, Gray volunteered to clean up so Rachel decided to call June. She'd gone to New York to visit her aging mother so Rachel hadn't seen her in nearly two weeks.

"June?"

"Oh heavens, Rachel! Where are you? I just heard your house was robbed and I drove by when I got back but you weren't there. What's going on around here?"

Rachel smiled into the phone. How she'd missed her friend!

"We're okay. My house was broken into but nothing is missing. I think it was just a terrible prank. I'm taking care of things. Have you heard from Tilly?"

"Not a word. I drove by her place, too. Rachel, she's been evicted."

"I know." Rachel pressed her forehead against the kitchen cupboard and sighed. "I reported her missing to the police yesterday."

They were both quiet for a moment. Then June said, "I always warned her that something like this would happen. But she never listened. She loved her men."

Rachel's chest ached. "The cashier at Pat's said Jay's been reported missing, too."

June made a hissing sound. "I been in this town the whole of sixty years and we've never had a single person turn up missing, except your friend Savannah when she got stuck in that underground room. And now there's two more of them!"

"Both co-workers." Rachel added softly. "Do you think Jim's involved?"

"Bah. He's too old. Besides, he liked Tilly. It's the only reason that girl still had a job, what with all her shenanigans," June pointed out.

"It's got to be Carl, then."

"He's a weenie."

"Yes, but he's a weenie with a bad temper," Rachel reminded her.

"That's true," June conceded.

"Be careful, June."

"Oh, don't worry about me. I haven't pissed anyone off in a long time," she reassured Rachel with a laugh.

"What should we do about Tilly? Do you know if her family's been contacted?"

"I don't even know where to find her family," June returned. "Did she ever tell you anything about her past?"

"You, of all people, should know that I don't ask."

"And I've always respected you for that. Let the police take care of Tilly. Chief Mobely will track her down."

Chapter 20

Sunday dawned cool and sunny, feeling very much like autumn. Rachel dragged Anna to church, and then hurried home to spend time with Gray, and Mike when he was free. The next day Anna would start school, and any day now Mike's sting would take place, presumably bringing an end to the case. Feeling the clock ticking, she was determined to make the most of what little time they had left together.

Rachel watched a movie with Anna and then prepared a roast for dinner that evening. At dinner, Anna chattered endlessly about school the next day, giving her parents and Gray a blessed distraction from worrying about the upcoming sting. The girl didn't seem to notice the tension in the air while she covered everything from what she'd chosen to wear, to what she thought about each of her subjects.

After dinner, Rachel asked Anna to help her clear the table and make a lunch for the next day while Mike and his father moved into the living room to talk. Mike and Gary had been so busy over the last two days that it seemed like Rachel only saw him at bedtime. Then she had his undivided attention.

Once the kitchen was cleared from dinner, Rachel sent Anna to take a shower and joined Mike in the living room. Gray had just gone to bed.

"Is everything ready?" Rachel asked quietly as she sat on the couch next to Mike. He put an arm around her shoulders and pulled her tight against him.

"Once the warrants come through we'll put on one last show and then this will all be over. By the end of the week I plan to have Jim, Carl *and* Ricky in jail." Hearing that Anna was done in the shower, Mike changed the subject. "The dinner you made tonight was incredible. I probably won't make it home for dinner tomorrow night, but what about Tuesday? Are you going to make anything special for dinner Tuesday night?"

Her heart thrilled to his hopeful tone. "Uh, how about an apple on the run? Anna has try-outs after school and Gray and I are going to watch."

"What's she trying out for?"

Rachel closed her eyes. "Hockey."

"No kidding? That's great!"

"I knew you'd see it that way," she grumbled.

"What's wrong with hockey?"

"It's an expensive sport. And she hasn't had a lot of practice."

"She'll do fine. If the coach is any good, he'll know what to look for. Text me the location and I'll try to make it. Oh, and don't worry about the cost. I'll take care of it."

Indignation made her heart pound. "You don't have to pay, Mike. We've managed all these years without handouts." Her throat closed up and she couldn't continue. She was embarrassed at her outburst.

"It's not a handout," he growled. "It's my first chance to do something for my own kid." He paused for a moment. "And when the arrests are behind us we're going to talk about that."

"Yes, I agree."

"I want my name on her birth certificate."

Rachel opened her mouth to respond to that unexpected demand when Anna came into the living room. Rachel jumped away from Mike. Rolling his eyes at her, Mike gave her a quick squeeze and got up to speak to Anna.

"Good luck on your first day of school, Anna. I might not be here to hear all about it, but know that I'll be thinking about you all day, okay? Good night, sweetie." He ruffled her hair making her scrunch her nose.

"Go brush your teeth, honey, and I'll come in to lay with you in a few minutes."

"Can Grandpa go with us to take me to school tomorrow?" Anna asked.

"We'll ask him in the morning."

The girl nodded and headed into the bathroom to get ready for bed while Rachel double checked that her backpack was packed and her clothes were laid out. She poked her head into Mike's room to say goodnight but he was already on the phone so she settled for a quick wave and closed the door quietly. Minutes later both she and Anna were asleep.

After taking Anna to school the next morning, Rachel dropped Gray off at the library just a few blocks from Mike's house and headed to her shift at the museum. She picked him up again in time to be at school when the classes let out. Anna's smile proved she had a great first day of school.

"How was your first day?" Gray asked Anna while she hooked her seatbelt and settled her backpack on the seat next to her.

"It was great!" Anna chirped. She consumed a lot of the drive and most of the evening talking about homework and teachers and what everyone else had done all summer long. By bedtime, Anna had nearly talked herself out, so Rachel had little trouble getting her into bed.

"Aren't you coming to lay down with me?" Anna asked when Rachel took a step toward the hallway.

"In a minute, Anna. I just want to walk through one last time and make sure everything is ready for tomorrow."

"Ok," Anna yawned. "But hurry."

Rachel nodded at Anna and closed the door behind her. As she'd told Anna, she checked that the doors were locked, and that Anna's backpack and clothes were ready for the morning. Missing Mike, Rachel sat on the edge of his bed thinking to spend a few minutes in peace, but when she woke in his bed on Tuesday morning, she found another little note he'd left her during the night.

Miss you, baby. See you soon.

Rachel drew a heart on the note and placed it back under his pillow and then went into the spare bedroom to wake Anna. The second day of school was a little less exciting to Anna and so Rachel had a harder time getting her motivated in the morning.

"You've got to eat something for breakfast, cutie."

Anna yawned and dropped her chin on her hand as she leaned over the little kitchen table. "I'm too tired to eat."

Rachel rolled her eyes. "It's only been one day. You can't be exhausted yet." She set a bowl of cereal in front of her which the girl dug into right away. After dropping Anna off at school, Gray once again headed to the library and Rachel went through Mike's house, cleaning and gathering her and Anna's things. In a couple of days they could be back in their own house again.

As she was putting Anna's laundry away, she came across the scrapbook that Anna had kept of her father. It wasn't much to look at as far as scrapbooks go. It was a small four by six photo album that held a few grainy cut out pictures of Mike cut from the college paper. Rachel was partly embarrassed that she'd been so enamored of him back then that she'd saved those pictures but a larger part was glad that she'd kept them for they had been Anna's only link to her daddy.

Perhaps she should take some pictures of Anna with Mike and Gray before they left so that Anna would have something new to add to her album. That thought led to another. How would Anna react to finding out that Mike was her father? They would have to tell her soon before someone slipped, just as soon as the case was over.

Anna would be thrilled, for sure. But how would she be impacted by their leaving? Rachel knew that Mike and Gray would stay in touch now that they knew about Anna. But how could she help Anna to understand this dynamic? Her family awareness probably only covered married parents and divorced parents with joint custody. Anna's parents were neither. What a mess Rachel had made of things!

She put the album back in Anna's suitcase and heard the front door slam. There were footsteps and then, "Mom?"

"In your room, sweetie," Rachel called.

"Wow! It looks so clean in here." Anna wandered around the room examining the shelves and closet.

"Ha! It could look like this all the time if you picked up after yourself. Mike would probably appreciate that."

Anna shrugged. "Mike likes me just the way I am. Are you ready? Grandpa is waiting in the living room."

Rachel sent a text to Mike as soon as they arrived at the rink in neighboring Black River and took their seats. When he didn't respond after a few minutes, she stowed her phone and settled in to watch the practice.

She and Gray watched from the stands as the kids filed out onto the ice. She scanned the group trying to pick out Anna beneath all the safety equipment they were wearing. Her heart skipped a beat when she spotted Mike making his way up the steps toward them. He looked good in a white T-shirt that was just tight enough to show off his muscular chest and tattooed arms and low-slung worn jeans. She felt her mouth go dry when he grinned at her. He gave her a quick hard kiss and then dropped into the seat on her right. "Did I miss her?" He looked down the row and nodded a greeting at his father.

"They just came out. They haven't started any of the exercises yet," Gray reported.

Rachel turned her attention back to the ice. "I haven't figured out which one she is yet."

"She's wearing the nine jersey." Mike barely glanced at the rest of the group.

Rachel looked down at the child he indicated and frowned. "She looks so tiny."

"She'll be fine."

Anna skated to the center of the rink on surprisingly stable legs considering the weight of the gear she had on and they watched as the coach took her through a few basic maneuvers. Beside her, Mike smiled.

"She's really good." He looked over at Rachel and her breath hitched when she recognized the pride in his eyes. "Do you take her skating?"

Rachel shrugged. "A few times. She took to it pretty quickly."

"It's hereditary," Gray added.

Between them, Rachel rolled her eyes but she couldn't help but be pleased with their obvious admiration of the girl. Mike and his father narrated the practice, most of which was foreign to Rachel. When practice was over they stood to cheer for Anna as the children left the ice.

"If the coach doesn't put her on the team I'll give him a call," Mike was telling Gray as they headed down to the lobby.

"He will," Gray told him. "She skates just like you did at that age. The girl's a natural."

"Don't you dare intervene if she doesn't make the cut," Rachel interrupted. "You can't solve every problem she has. Not making the team will build character. She'll live."

Mike furrowed his brow. "She already has character. Loads of it."

Rachel opened her mouth to argue but Anna bounced up just then. "Did you see me, Mom? It was so much fun. I think I was pretty good, too. The coach said he'll post the team in a couple of days." She beamed at her little audience.

"You were great!" Mike told her. He rested a hand on her shoulder and steered her toward the parking lot.

"My daddy played hockey," she told him.

"I've heard that."

"Did you hear how good he was? He won a championship. I bet he'd be proud if he knew."

Behind them, Rachel saw Mike's shoulders stiffen. "I know he would."

"I'll work hard. I want to make him proud of me."

Mike half-turned and met Rachel's eyes. "I bet he already is."

Anna spun around and walked backward. "Can I ride home with Mike?"

Mike looked backed at Rachel again and smiled.

"Sure, honey."

"Yay!" Anna ran to Mike's Charger and waited by the door.

Gray walked with Rachel to her car. He was quiet as they got in and headed home. Rachel had the impression he was considering his next words so she didn't try to fill the silence with talk. As they neared Mike's house, Gray placed a hand on her arm.

"Rachel." His voice was quiet and laced with emotion. "I've given this a lot of thought, and I'd like to ask you something. I don't know if you and Mike have discussed what you'll tell Anna, but when the case is over I'd like to stay on in Wolf Creek and continue being her grandpa." He removed his hand and looked at Mike's house as they pulled into the driveway. "I really like it here. And you two are here." He gave her a smile that she thought looked a little sad. "If it's not too presumptuous of me, I'd like us to be a family." Rachel frowned but he continued. "Regardless of what becomes of you and Mike, you'll both always be part of my family now."

She nodded once and was surprised when a sob escaped. He patted her arm and opened his door. "You can think about it and let me know." He left her in the car to recover herself and went to Anna and Mike who had pulled in ahead of them.

Rachel checked her face in the visor mirror and then got out. Anna had gone straight into the house but Mike waited for her and was checking messages on his phone when she drew up to his side. She started to move past him, but he stowed his phone in his pocket and snaked a hand out to pull her to him. He buried his face in her neck and settled his arms around her waist. "I miss you when I'm away," he mumbled, letting his lips trail along her jawbone until he reached her mouth.

She let herself melt into his embrace and admitted, "I miss you too." She felt him smile against her lips.

Mike took her hand and they walked into the house together. Stopping just inside the door, Rachel took in the scatter of Anna's school things that already spanned the kitchen and living room.

"We've completely taken over your house, Mike. Just as soon as you give the okay, Anna and I can go home."

"What's the rush?" He squeezed her hand. "I love playing house with you."

"We all need to get back to our normal lives, Mike. I have a reputation to repair." When he looked confused, she explained. "Apparently, we're causing quite a stir. They're even gossiping about me at Pat's."

"The grocery store?" He looked incredulous so she recapped the conversation she'd had with the cashier.

"Hmm. Okay. We'll —" He broke off as his phone rang. "It's Gary."

Rachel motioned that she was heading in the other room to give him some privacy.

Mike went into his bedroom and stayed there until well after Anna had gone to bed. Rachel looked up from the couch when he poked his head in to get her attention. He nodded toward the bedroom so she got up and followed him with a quick apology to Gray for deserting him. Gray waved a hand and went back to the investigative medical show they'd been watching together.

She closed the bedroom door behind her and waited while he fired up his laptop. When he turned apologetic eyes on her, she shivered. Something had happened. "This is about Tilly, isn't it?"

"Two bodies were found."

Rachel swallowed but the lead in her stomach threatened to push its way to her throat as she thought about that. It had to be Jay. The police's informant. Dead. Things like this only happened in movies and big cities. They didn't happen in Wolf Creek, population 2,000. Mike reached out and held her hands in his.

"I'm meeting Gary at the reservation."

Chapter 21

"A couple of hikers found her around 3 p.m." Gary told him without preamble. Mike looked over the first body without expression. Gary blanched. "Whoever did that to her has serious anger issues."

Mike nodded but his thoughts were on Rachel. The battered, bloated woman lying in the shallow, rocky grave in front of them could have easily been her instead. He squeezed the phone in his hand, itching to call her.

Gary cocked his head to the side and studied the woman's face. "You think it's Tilly?"

Mike brought up a photo from Tilly's social page. He looked from the bright smile and inviting pose to the destroyed body below. She had been badly beaten and after days in the heat and elements, the woman's face was swollen and distorted. "Hard to tell."

"This one's got a tattoo." He pointed at the woman's partially exposed breast. "You see that?"

Mike squatted down near the corpse and looked at the mark. "Kind of looks like a heart, doesn't it?"

Gary shook his head. "She's got the tattoo of a heart over her heart? Seems redundant."

Mike didn't answer. He stood and flipped through the photos Tilly had posted on her page looking for evidence of the tattoo. He felt like a voyeur studying her chest in each picture. A few pictures were promising but nothing was clear enough for a positive identification.

While Gary talked to the crime scene team, Mike called Rachel. She picked up on the first ring. She sounded tired, but he knew she hadn't been asleep.

"Is it her?" She asked without preamble.

He lowered his voice. "No one has been identified yet. I should've probably asked you this before you left. Does Tilly have any piercings? Tattoos? Anything else memorable on her body that we can document?"

Rachel's indrawn breath reminded Mike that he probably should have been less truthful about the condition of the body.

"I don't know about piercings, but she had a tattoo. I never saw it–but I remember when she got it. A heart on her, you know, chest. Over her heart." Her voice cracked. "She said it was a reminder that the only person that would ever love her was herself." He heard a sniffle. "I'm sorry. Does–does one of them have a tattoo?

"I really can't talk about it yet." His voice was apologetic now. "But I'll let the authorities handling the case know. I'm sure it'll help."

"Mike? I'm not in danger, am I? I mean, could I be next?"

"You're safe. Nobody's out to hurt you." But they both knew his confidence was forced.

Her voice dropped to a whisper. "Could it have been Carl? Or Jim Charles?" She asked quietly.

"The crime scene unit is still processing the site for evidence but it's not as fast as it looks on TV. The DEA net is back in place. We're just waiting for Jimienez to show up in town. After the raid I'll have enough on Jim and Carl for indictments on several counts. Having their DNA to implicate them in these murders would be enough to put them away for life." Mike lowered his voice too. "It's almost over, baby. I promise."

"I know." Rachel's voice was heavy with emotion.

"It could get dangerous in town at night, especially at Suds. Do you or Anna have anything going tomorrow?"

"Just school. Your dad's taking her."

"Okay, good. I'll talk to him about picking her up too. Word about bodies found will get around fast. I'm sure it's going to put Jim and Carl on edge. And the fact that I'm in town again just when Jimienez is about to show up has them suspicious. They think I'm going to upstage them. It's possible Carl could try to use you to distract me."

"It won't work."

"It *would* work," Mike corrected her. "So to be safe, I want you to stick close to home tomorrow."

"My home? Or here?" Rachel asked.

"I wish I could say they were one and the same."

"I was going to move our things back tomorrow."

Mike thought for a minute. It would be convenient to use his house as a command center. And his job was definitely not something he wanted to expose Anna to. "Yeah, okay. But promise me you'll stay away from town."

"I promise. I'm not going to show my face in town again until well after you've gone. I can't take the scrutiny."

Rachel's voice was light, but Mike frowned. "A few more days. Then we'll be able to tell everyone that you're dating the hero." Mike meant it as a joke but Rachel's voice was pathetic when she responded.

"Except by then you'll be gone."

"I'll make it up to you, I promise. I've got to go, baby. See you later." He disconnected the call and returned to Gary's side to get an update on what the police technicians had found. By the time they talked to the chief and made notes of their own, it was well past midnight. Gary left to return to his hotel room and Mike hurried home.

Everything was dark when he let himself in, so he made his way silently through the house and into his bedroom, locking the bedroom door in case he'd somehow woken Anna. He paused to look at Rachel, sound asleep and hugging his pillow to her chest. She looked so peaceful, so exquisitely beautiful there waiting for him that his heart swelled with the love he felt for her. He wondered how she'd react to hearing his intention to stay in Wolf Creek. The idea of coming home to this, to Rachel and his daughter was so compelling that he nearly woke Rachel to tell her before coming to his senses and reminding himself that his declarations had to wait until the case was over, until they were safe from the clutches of drugs and violence that permeated Wolf Creek.

Rachel woke when the mattress dipped beside her. Mike was seated beside her hip, tugging off his jeans and socks. She opened her eyes to find him staring at her with an intensity that startled her. When she sat up to face him he tipped her chin up for a kiss. Reaching behind her he tugged the hem of her nightgown up over her head and onto the floor.

Rachel watched placidly as he settled in next to her. She loved being able to make love with him night after night. She'd always heard that doing something twenty-one times makes a habit and she wondered if that applied to sex. That thought led to another and suddenly her insides went cold. Her period was late. She counted back in her head. Oh yes. She was four weeks late.

Mike brought his hands up to her shoulders when he felt her go still. "What's the matter?"

She blinked at him. This was definitely not the time to bring up a possible pregnancy. Not when he was on the verge of a drug sting. She shook herself and tried to relax. There would be time to tell him later. "I guess I just got distracted. I can't believe it's almost over."

"You'll get your life back." He smiled but she couldn't bring herself to return it.

Could she really be pregnant...again? How was that even possible? She was on the Pill and she'd never missed it. Except the night she'd had the migraine and Mike had taken back to his house instead of taking her home. And then again a few days later, the first time they'd made love. Her stomach rolled and clenched tight. She tried to calm her breathing. He'd asked about protection and she'd promised him she was covered. Would he think she was trying to trap him?

"Babe?"

"Yeah. I guess so." She mumbled and tried to lighten the mood. "I'm kind of getting used to having you guys around to help with Anna when I'm working. I'm going to miss that."

He pulled her to him again, not in passion this time, but with something more tender. "I wish I could have helped you with Anna."

"I know." She sighed. His skin was warm and she was so tired. She yawned. "Right now, we're in your way. Tomorrow night you'll get your bed back." When Mike laid down she settled back into the bed and curled up against him.

"I like it better with you in it."

They made love leisurely, savoring every touch, every emotion, both of them knowing that once the head of the drug cartel arrived in Wolf Creek, things were going to get crazy.

The next morning Gray took Anna to school while Mike and Gary met to go over the plan one last time. Once arrests were made Mike wanted both Ricky and Big Jim transferred to a federal prison right away and he needed to make sure no judge would allow them to post bail. There were a lot of details to cover.

When Gary left to brief Bill Mobely one last time before that evening, Gray wandered into the kitchen where Mike was hovering over his laptop.

"I got Anna to school and spoke with the principal in case I need to pick her up early." He paused. "So after tonight this case will be over?" Gray leaned back against the countertop and looked at his son.

"Assuming we make the arrests tonight I'll have to go back to D.C. again for a few weeks to go over everything with the prosecutors."

Gray nodded. He was familiar with the process from Mike's previous cases. "I'm going to stay, if you don't mind."

Mike was distracted but he dipped his head. "Yeah. I don't mind."

"No, what I mean is that I'm going to move here. Buy a house even."

Mike's head came up, then he looked over at his father.

"Unless there's a reason, a damn good reason, that you don't want me to be a part of their lives," he tipped his head toward the bedroom Anna had claimed as her own, "I'd like to stay and be a part of their family."

Mike grinned. "Funny. I had the same intention." He ran a hand through his hair. "I guess the population of Wolf Creek just increased by two."

Gray smiled. "Have you told Rachel yet?"

Mike frowned. "No, but I'm sure she's figured it out by now."

"Don't be so sure about that. I think she's still under the impression that you're leaving when this is over."

"I'll straighten her out soon enough."

"Don't screw this up," Gray warned. They both knew what Gray was thinking. Mike's mother had only been gone a year. Having a grandchild meant a lot to Gray and he was afraid Mike would do something to jeopardize that relationship.

"I don't intend to," Mike promised.

Rachel woke late to find the house empty. It was after ten a.m. so she assumed that everyone was out doing what they needed for the sting that night. She made coffee and wrestled with a bout of nausea as she waited for it to brew. She couldn't decide whether the illness was prompted by her suspicion of being pregnant or from actually being pregnant. She realized that she'd been feeling off for a few weeks but had attributed it to the stress of living in a different house and worrying about Mike.

Mike came into the house just as the coffee was finishing so she poured him a cup, accepted a kiss in return and then sipped her own as she leaned back against the counter, watching him work. The coffee stopped threatening to boil back up her throat. She looked up when the door opened again.

Gary closed the door behind him and looked from Mike at the table in front of his computer, to Rachel. "Well, isn't this cozy? I feel like I'm intruding on your domestic bliss."

Mike and Rachel shared a quick look.

"It's nice to see you, Gary," Rachel said to ease the tension.

"And you. You look a little pale. Feeling okay?"

Rachel's stomach chose that moment to reject the coffee and she ran for the bathroom.

She heard Gary ask Mike, "Something I said? I was only teasing her."

"She's probably just nervous. I'll go check on her."

Rachel hadn't closed the bathroom door all the way so Mike was treated to a view of her huddled over the toilet, heaving up the few sips of coffee she'd swallowed. He leaned against the doorframe. "Are you okay?"

She put the lid down, flushed the toilet and sat on it. He could see that she was shaking. "I think so. I feel a little better now."

"Anything I can do for you?"

She shook her head. "I might go lie down for a little while. I was going to pack up our things and take them back to my house today."

He held a hand out to stop her. "Rachel."

"Anna and I need to get out of the way. And we need to get back to our normal lives."

"I love having you here."

She looked at her hands. She was twisting her fingers and now they were an angry red. "It's time."

Gary peeked his head around the corner. "Mike?"

"I'm coming," he told Gary, his eyes never leaving Rachel's face. "Go lie down. I'll check on you before we go."

"Your dad will be back soon?"

"He should be."

Mike followed Gary out to the kitchen so Rachel scurried into Mike's bathroom where her toothbrush was. She splashed water on her face and brushed her teeth and then climbed into his big, comfy bed.

As promised, Mike came in to let her know when he and Gary were leaving. She rolled onto her back and studied his face. Her stomach clenched again but this time she knew it was because she was worried about him. He looked confident, excited even, but then he did this all the time. The concern for his safety and the realization that she still loved him so very much left her weak. "You'll be careful?"

He gave her the familiar cocky smile that she'd first fallen for in college. "I'm always careful, babe." His smile slid from his face as he sat on the bed next to her. He placed a hand on her hip and rubbed it gently. "If everything goes as planned tonight Gary and I will be leaving tomorrow to get these jerks locked up. We'll then have to head to D.C. to give depositions and work with the prosecutors. The minute that's finished,

I'll be coming back here and we're going to work some things out."

"About Anna," Rachel assumed.

"Yes, definitely Anna. But also with us."

Rachel looked away from him, willing her tears to stay in their place. Before she could think of the right response, he leaned down and kissed her sweetly.

"Lay low today. I need to know you're safe. I've asked my dad to stay close to the school. Anna's probably not in any danger, but I won't take any chances with her."

"Thank you," Rachel whispered.

Rachel took a quick, reviving shower after Mike and Gary left. Then she packed up her and Anna's things. It took her three trips to get their bags loaded into her old car and then she took one last look around to be sure they hadn't left anything behind.

She felt sad leaving. Mike's house was comfortable and having their company had been more than nice. Of course, Gray had declared his intention to stay and that brought a smile to her lips. Anna would be elated to learn he was her real grandfather!

Rachel locked up the house and drove out of her way to a little party store where she would be less likely to run into someone she knew. She bought a pregnancy test, a gallon of milk and a loaf of bread. By the time she got to her own house she was almost convinced she was happy about a hypothetical baby. Another thought hit her as soon as she unlocked the door. Would Mike feel obligated to stay if he knew he was about to have another child? She didn't want him to resent that intrusion in his life. He would be a great father, he was proving that already. But what if he didn't want her for the long term? It was obvious that he liked having her around and living together for the past weeks had been easy, but love? He'd never used the words. Neither had she, she scolded herself.

She stowed the milk and bread in the refrigerator and then held the box in her hands. Ten years later her life was very nearly back where it had started, on the brink of significant change. Just as soon as she worked up the nerve, she would find out.

Chapter 22

Mike knew the exact moment Ricky Jimienez hit town and he was in the bar waiting on his chance to catch Jim and Ricky together. Knowing Big Bill's penchant for showboating, Mike figured he would bring Ricky to Suds N Grub before the exchange. Gary was positioned in an adjacent parking lot, keeping an eye on their cars and looking for any other suspicious activity.

It would have been convenient to have Rachel working tonight, to be his eyes and ears inside that private dining room, but there was no way Mike would risk her life so he asked her to call in sick. In fact, if there was any way to close down the whole bar without blowing his cover, he would have done it. Until Ricky and Jim, and even Carl were behind bars, no one in Wolf Creek was safe.

The team spent the majority of the day keeping tabs on all three men. The jackpot would be to find them together with the drugs, but they had the resources to take them separately if it came to that.

Just as he had predicted, Big Jim brought Ricky into Suds after happy hour and made a big deal of offering him drinks on the house. Mike kept an eye on them from his spot at the bar but he noted with some frustration that Carl wasn't there. He relayed this to Gary who had one of the team drive by his house. He wasn't there either. That left nearly a dozen other places Carl could be, all of them too public for a takedown. He knew from their dealings that both Jim and Carl carried a concealed weapon and neither would hesitate to use it if he was cornered. No, they needed to wait and see if Carl would show later.

Gary checked in occasionally to report the team's status while Mike sat at the bar, drinking a beer and watching the boisterous crowd. He texted his father to be sure that Rachel and Anna were safe. Gray reported that they'd returned to their own house for the night but that he made sure they were locked up tight before he left. He promised to take Anna to school in the morning and signed off with a reminder to stay safe which gave Mike a laugh. Once a father, always a father he supposed.

Around closing time Big Jim left the back room with a watchful Ricky Jimienez in tow. They shouldered their way through the dancers and left through the front door. Mike texted Gary to be ready for them and then paid his tab with the bartender.

Mike drove around for the next two hours, waiting for the signal. Around four a.m. he stopped at the gas station and got himself a coffee. This fruitless waiting was always his least favorite part of any operation. He was just getting back into his car when a text came in from Gary. The coded message was what they used when they needed the other to call from somewhere private. He dialed Gary immediately.

Wasting no time on preliminaries, Gary reported the status. "We've got the net in place, just waiting on you."

"All three of them?"

"Just Jim and Ricky. No sign of Carl. But this is it — as good as it's going to get, Mike. Get over here."

Mike threw his car in gear and sped to the spot they'd selected to watch the transaction take place. Creeping through the wooded lot to a clearing a safe distance from the designated drop site, Mike joined Bill Mobely and Gary as they waited for the semi's doors to open revealing the largest drug drop in Wolf Creek history.

They waited for the moment Ricky picked up a brick of wrapped white substance and signaled the strike team to move in. Within in minutes they had both men and the truck driver in custody. The next few hours were spent on the arrest and transfer of the criminals and then processing the scene and moving the evidence to a secure location. By the time the sting was wrapped up, it was almost nine a.m., nearly twenty-four hours since it had begun.

Mike texted Gray and Rachel to let them both know that it was over and that he was safe. In his mind, it was imperative that they find Carl right away because now that Big Jim and Ricky had been arrested, Mike's cover, and Rachel's assumed involvement in the sting would be exposed. She was in danger.

Mike was updating the local on duty officers with an ATL for Carl when Gray called Mike.

"What's going on?" Mike asked, knowing that his father would only call if there were an emergency.

"I just drove by Rachel's house again after taking Anna to school and there's another car in the driveway."

"Is her car there?"

"The garage door is down. I can't tell. Should I go in?"

"Stay where you are and stay on the phone. I'm on my way."

Mike ran for his car, threw it into gear and punched the gas. He was five minutes away. Gray's voice was low and worried. "I can see a man in there through the front window. In the kitchen maybe. Something's off about this Mike. It's not one of us and Rachel wouldn't have let anyone else in. I have a bad feeling."

"So do I," he growled as he pulled to a stop behind Gray's car. Gary pulled up right behind him. Mike signaled for his dad to stay in the car while he and Gary picked their way quietly across the neighbor's yard. They'd been partners long enough that they were able to communicate without words. They each took one side of the house and peeked in the windows. They met on the far side of the neighbor's house.

"Carl's got Rachel on a chair in the kitchen. Doesn't look like she's hurt but she still looks rough." Ice ran through Mike's veins as Gary cautioned him.

"She's okay, Mike. She was sick yesterday, right? That might be why she looks bad. She's safe enough for the moment. You can't go charging in there. Not yet."

Gary stood in front of Mike in case he decided to bolt while he called the chief to get officers to the house. "Let's go back and get into place, but I'm warning you—stay outside until reinforcements get here. Two minutes, Mike."

He nodded once to indicate he heard his partner, his jaw working furiously. They hurried back to Rachel's house and took up positions near the kitchen door. They waited until two officers and the chief arrived and positioned themselves at the other entrances. Radio countdown signaled the okay to enter.

Doors slammed and shouted orders filled the house just as Carl raised a hand to strike Rachel across the face. Mike entered ahead of his partner and took in the scene in a heartbeat. With a feral growl, he threw himself at Carl, knocking him to the ground and breaking her dining table in the process. When Carl fumbled for his gun, Mike threw one solid punch that knocked him out and then turned his attention to Rachel. As a deputy brought Carl around, Gary gave him the list of offenses for which he was being charged. Mike cut the zip-ties at Rachel's wrists and ankles to free her from her chair.

Rachel swiped at Mike's forehead the instant her hands were free. "You're hurt." A sob escaped and she pressed her hand to her mouth.

"I'm okay. Are you hurt?"

She shook her head and then wailed, "And you broke my table!"

A smile touched his lips as he tugged her into his arms. "We can replace the table, sweetheart," he whispered into her hair.

Gary came back into the kitchen after walking Carl out to the squad car and slapped Mike on the back with a smile. "That's all three down! Ready when you are."

Mike gave a nod. "I'll leave for D.C. later today or early tomorrow. I'm going to stay while Rachel is interviewed."

Gary turned his smile to Rachel. "Glad you're okay. Hopefully the next time we'll meet under better circumstances, eh?"

"Yes."

Rachel waited while Mike spoke with Chief Mobely. Mike promised to follow him to the police station with Rachel as soon as she was ready.

"We'll be just a minute behind you," Rachel told the chief. "I want to have a look at the cut on Mike's head first."

Once everyone left Mike followed Rachel to the bathroom but stopped her in the doorway. "I'm so sorry I wasn't here. Are you sure you weren't hurt?"

"I'm not hurt. You got here in time. I should have listened to you and stayed at your house today. I'm so sorry, Mike. I just wanted to get out of your way but Carl came here looking for me when I called in sick."

"I was so worried when my dad called me. This could have gone to hell so quickly. I could have lost you." The hand he put to her cheek was shaking.

Rachel blinked at him. "Mike."

"I love you, Rachel. You and Anna." He looked at the floor and back into her eyes. "You have no idea how hard I looked for you after that semester. I was ready to report you missing."

She managed a smile. "I'm glad you didn't."

"I wish I had. I might have found you sooner."

She smiled at him, relief and joy glowing on her face.

"Now that I've found you, I don't plan to let you go," he warned.

Her face clouded. "This is the only home Anna has ever known. I can't uproot her."

Mike pulled her back into his arms. "My father tells me he's declared his intention to settle in Wolf Creek. If this is where my family lives, how could I live anywhere else?"

Rachel looked up into his eyes. "I love you, Mike. I've loved you since the first day I met you. I've never slept with, never even dated anyone else." She gave a small laugh. "Not because I ever thought I'd get you back some day but because no one could compare to you."

He kissed her sweetly, not with passion but with a depth of emotion that defied words. She started to thread a hand through his hair and seemed to remember the gash on his head.

"Let's get you fixed up. The chief's expecting us." She took two steps into the bathroom and stopped short. The pregnancy test she'd taken after Anna left for school was still lying on the countertop.

Mike felt her hesitation and glanced around for the cause. He spotted the stick on the counter and approached it slowly as if it could explode at any moment. Rachel stood frozen to the spot so he had to reach past her to pick it up. His heart pounded when he looked at it. "What does a plus mean?"

He looked from the test to Rachel. Their eyes locked.

"Are you kidding me?" His voice cracked.

She managed a weak nod. "We did it again." Her expression was solemn.

Mike's face split into a wide grin as he snatched her off the ground and swung her around. "We're having a baby?" He set her down and looked at her with a little bit of awe.

"You're happy about this?" She asked in a voice barely louder than a whisper.

"I'm thrilled." He paused. "Aren't you?"

"I hadn't really considered there could be a happy ending for us."

"Well, there is. And just as soon as we are finished at the police station I'll set about proving it to you. Both of you—all of you," he amended. "My mom must be beaming in heaven right now."

"Maybe she arranged the whole thing?" Rachel teased.

They discussed how to tell Anna about Mike and then about the baby as she cleaned and bandaged his cut. Mike decided he'd never been so thankful for a migraine in his life. Then they headed to the police station so that Rachel could give her report.

At their instruction, Gray took Anna to Mike's house after school and got her started on her homework. Mike and Rachel arrived shortly afterward with suitcases and two pizzas. Anna spotted her suitcase and turned suspicious eyes on her mother. "I thought we couldn't stay here anymore."

Rachel looked at Anna and then at Gray's matching expression. "How would you like to stay a little longer?"

"Yes!" She hopped out of her seat and hugged her mom while Mike carried the suitcases to the bedrooms. When he returned Rachel saw that he was holding Anna's scrapbook and something else bundled up in his arms. Their eyes met.

"Anna," Rachel began. "What's your deepest wish?"

Anna looked confused and Rachel knew that she was wondering why her mother was asking a question she already knew the answer to. "To have a family. To have you and my daddy," she gave Mike a quick apologetic look, "together. I want a mom and a dad and a brother or sister."

"What about a Grandpa?" Gray teased.

Anna beamed at him. "I have you."

Gray grinned back at her. "You sure do."

Mike held out her scrapbook, open to a newsprint picture of him in his hockey jersey. "Is this your dad?"

Anna nodded. "Yes, that's him." She put her finger on his face in the picture in case he was referring to someone else.

Mike unfolded the garment in his arms. Anna looked from the jersey he held to the one in the picture.

"Where did you get that?" She asked in awe.

"It's mine, Anna. That's me in your picture." He watched her as she took in that news.

"You're my daddy?" She looked to her mom for confirmation. "My real daddy?"

Rachel nodded. "Mike is your daddy. And Gray is your real grandpa."

Anna squealed and threw herself into Mike's arms. The tears in his eyes brought tears to Rachel's. "Now I just need a brother or sister and my wish will come true."

Mike laughed and set her down. "I've put in the order. Do you think you can wait until the spring?"

Anna's eyes got huge. "Yes!"

Above Anna's head Rachel met Gray's eyes and she gave him a subtle nod. Fresh tears came to everyone, but Anna was oblivious.

"Well," Gray stood and wiped his face. "This calls for a pizza celebration!"

Mike flew to D.C. the next morning, after leaving his girls with a promise that he'd be back for good in a few days.

For Rachel, the days felt too long with Mike gone and no full-time job to go to. Suds N Grub would remain closed until after the trial and Savannah was out of town for a conference.

Anna was all too happy to go to school and tell everyone who would listen about her new family, but Rachel doubted many people believed her. It was, after all, a pretty incredible story.

Gray enlisted Rachel's help in looking for a house to purchase. On Saturday, Anna went with them as they drove around looking for just the right place. Mike called to apologize that he was held up an extra day.

Sunday morning Rachel got a late start because of her morning sickness and then had to rush Anna to get ready for church. This, of course, made Anna grouchy. Gray surveyed the scene patiently from the front door as he waited for them to get their shoes on.

"Are you sure you know what you signed on for?" Rachel asked with one eyebrow raised. She hadn't meant to sound snotty, but she was feeling sick and frustrated.

"Loving every minute, even the grouchy ones." he assured her.

Hearts on the Run

They got to church on time thanks to Gray's skillful coaxing. Rachel was amused to see a few of the older ladies sit up straighter and primp their hair as Gray led them to a seat near the front. She pulled out the worship bulletin and was looking it over when a hush fell over the congregation. She looked up and around just as Anna gave an excited bounce. Mike was coming up the aisle toward them, only it was a very different version of Mike than the residents of Wolf Creek had seen before. This was the Mike she hadn't seen since college. Gone was his scruffy hair and unshaven face, his tattoos covered by a long sleeve shirt and tie. This Mike looked like the wealthy playboy son of a renowned heart surgeon, but in that moment she didn't care. She felt all eyes in church settle on them as he took his seat between Rachel and Anna.

"Hi Daddy!" She beamed.

"Hi Baby."

Anna's smile was contagious. Rachel could almost feel the women in the row behind them lean forward in their seats to capture every bit of their conversation.

"I missed you," Mike told Rachel, pulling her forward for a chaste kiss.

"We wanted you to come home yesterday," Anna scolded him.

He tore his eyes away from Rachel. "I had to make a quick detour."

"For what?"

"I stopped at my townhouse and packed up all of my stuff. I put it all into a truck and drove it back here."

"What about your cat?"

Mike cracked a smile. "I put her in a box on the seat next to me. She's not a fan of the highway."

Rachel raised her eyebrows. "You drove here from D.C. last night?"

"Drove all night," he confirmed. He exchanged a quick look with his father. "It suddenly seemed important that I give you this." He slipped a stunning two carat diamond ring onto her finger.

She could see that the gold was worn and her heart constricted painfully. She folded her hand and clutched it to her heart. "This was your mother's," she whispered. He nodded.

"I love it." She breathed.

Mike looked down at Anna, "And I needed to give you this." He dangled a gold chain in front of her. The charm was a series of interlinked hearts. "This belonged to your grandma and she would have wanted you to have it."

Like her mother, Anna clutched it and then dutifully turned so that Mike could fasten it around her neck. She wore it proudly all through church and a few times Rachel had to remind her to stop fiddling with it. She laughed softly to herself when she realized she'd been doing the same thing with her ring.

Hearts on the Run

After church she had the pleasure of introducing Mike and Gray to some of the congregation and seeing the looks of relief and acceptance on the faces of people that just a week earlier had shown concern or disdain.

Savannah and Daniel caught up with them in the parking lot. Daniel shook Mike's hand. "It's good to see you again."

"You, too."

"Case closed, huh?"

"Just about," Mike agreed.

Savannah gave Mike a quick hug. "I feel so bad for giving Rachel a hard time about you."

"I told you to trust me and leave it alone but you didn't listen," Daniel reminded her.

"I never listen to you!" she retorted, making everyone laugh. "You should have tried harder."

"Next time I'll put duct tape over your mouth," Daniel assured her.

She rolled her eyes at him. She turned to Mike. "I'm sorry for judging you, Mike. Welcome to Wolf Creek."

"Don't worry about it. You were supposed to judge me. I had to make everyone believe I was just as bad as the guys Big Jim dealt with in order to pull this off."

"Well, believe me when I say that I am totally relieved to find out you're not dangerous after all."

"Oh, he's dangerous all right," Daniel interrupted. "But he just happens to be dangerous on the right side of the law."

"Well, lucky for us then." She turned to Rachel and gave her a hug. "I'm so happy for you."

Gray insisted on driving Anna home so that Rachel could ride with Mike.

"Do you mind making one more stop before we go home?" Mike asked.

Home. She loved that sound. "Sure. Where to?"

"Pat's."

She squinted at him but his expression didn't give anything away. "You want to stop for groceries? It's too late for condoms." She added, making him laugh. "What do you need?"

He shrugged. "Don't know yet, but I'm sure I'll know it when I see it."

"You are so weird," she teased.

Mike grabbed a basket and wandered up and down the aisles picking seemingly random things from the shelves. When he was apparently satisfied with his selections, she followed him to the checkout. He chose a line that already had two customers even though the next lane was shorter.

She waited quietly beside him, knowing him well enough to understand that he was there for a reason. The purpose became clear a few minutes later when the cashier's eyes grew wide as she recognized them. Mike held Rachel's hand, playing with the ring on her finger as the cashier scanned the groceries and chattered on about Mike's role in the drug bust. Tears sprang to Rachel's eyes as she at last understood his game. He'd gone to the grocery store to start a new rumor in town.

"I love you so much," she told him on the way to the car. "You've made my life complete."

"Funny," Mike answered, pulling into his side for a kiss. "I was just about to say the same to you."

Epilogue

One Year Later

Mike pulled four-month-old, Alex, out of his highchair and settled him against his shoulder.

"Rachel! Anna!" He called up the stairs. "You're going to be late."

Anna appeared first, followed by Rachel. Mike kissed each of his girls, then to be funny, he placed a loud smacking kiss on his son's cheek as well.

"Where's Grandpa?" Anna wanted to know.

"He went jogging and then he's having coffee with Miss Sheila from the library."

"I thought he was taking me to school."

Mike grinned. "I'm taking you." He stepped back to include his wife as well. "Who's ready for their first day of school?"

"I am!" Anna chirped. "What about you, mom?"

Mike used his free arm to pull Rachel in for a kiss, making Anna groan. "You've got this, honey. We're all in your corner."

Rachel gave him a smile. "I'm just nervous. I haven't been to school in a long time."

"It's just like riding a bike," Mike teased.

Rachel smoothed Alex's fly-away hair. "I seem to recall that the last time you said that we ended up with him."

Mike laughed.

Anna frowned. "I don't get it."

Mike turned Anna toward the door. "Let's go you big sixth grader." Mike held the door while Alex babbled away. "Let's go Doctor Mommy."

Rachel paused in front of Mike where Alex promptly grabbed a handful of her hair and tried to put it in his mouth. "Have I told you lately how much I love you?"

Mike grinned. "It's been at least five minutes and I was starting to worry." He pressed a quick kiss to her forehead. "I'm so proud of you, Rachel. Go knock 'em dead."

Made in the USA
Columbia, SC
10 April 2022